FROM
ANOTHER
WORLD

FROM ANOTHER WORLD

Ana Maria Machado

Translated by
Luisa Baeta

•

With illustrations by
Lúcia Brandão

GROUNDWOOD BOOKS
HOUSE OF ANANSI PRESS
TORONTO BERKELEY

Groundwood Books / House of Anansi Press
110 Spadina Avenue, Suite 801, Toronto, Ontario M5V 2K4
or c/o Publishers Group West
1700 Fourth Street, Berkeley, CA 94710

Library and Archives Canada Cataloging in Publication
Machado, Ana Maria
From Another World / Ana Maria Machado; illustrated by Lúcia Brandão; translated
by Luisa Baeta.
Translation of: Do outro mundo.
ISBN 978-0-88899-597-1 (bound).–ISBN 978-0-88899-641-1 (pbk.)
1. Slavery–Juvenile fiction. I. Brandão, Lúcia II. Baeta, Luisa III. Title.
PZ7.M1795Fr 2005   j869.3'42   C2004-906129-1

Printed in Canada

MIX
Paper from
responsible sources
FSC® C004071

ANCIENT FOREST ™
FRIENDLY

To Veronica,
who told me her great-grandfather's history,
my starting point.

CONTENTS

1 Coffee and Milk   9

2 Someone Crying in the Night   25

3 Clear and Transparent   35

4 A Strange Conversation   47

5 Black Pieces, White Dots   53

6 Iaia's Candlestick   67

7 Black Beans and Rice   73

8 Black on White   87

9 All Right, I'll Write   105

History   133

Glossary   136

1

COFFEE AND MILK

PLEASE, excuse me. And be a bit patient. I'm not too good at this. I'm only writing – or trying to write – because I made a promise. Not an easy promise, a very solemn one. I gave my word.

So now I have to keep it.

To begin with I don't know how to begin. And I'm not sure I'll know how to end. But that will come later. For now I just have to begin. That's all.

I guess this is the best way to do it – as if I were talking, just telling my friends something. But I don't know if this is for one friend or for a lot of people I don't even know. I'm sorry if I'm acting weird, but I don't know much about books. Not like Elisa, Leo's sister. Be patient, you'll get to know them all soon enough.

To tell you the truth I could never bear to sit and read. I always found it very boring and tiring. I hated those rows of words on a page, those piles of pages inside the cover, all of them looking at me asking, "Ready? If you don't start now, there won't be time to read all of me before the quiz on Wednesday."

I didn't read a line at school if I could get away with it. I'd ask a friend to tell me the plot of a book and that was enough. Then when there was a test, I'd just try to answer the best I could.

I was always sure that I wouldn't need books in my life. After all, I'm going to study computers. I love computers. Numbers. The future. The world of tomorrow. Jobs where you can really make money. I bet I'm going to make a lot of money some day. And of course I won't need books for that. At least that's what I thought. Now I'm beginning to wonder a little. Just a little.

Anyway, all of this is just to let you know that I am not very excited about telling stories. But I was the chosen one. There's nothing I can do about it. Especially when I was chosen the way I was – from a past century, from another life. Or from another world. Who knows?

Well, that's what I'm going to tell you about. I'll stop beating around the bush. I haven't even told you how it all began.

First, let me introduce myself. My name is Mariano. I'm a normal guy, just like everyone else. I'm thin, I have dark hair, and now I'm wearing glasses. When the story happened – the story I'm about to tell you – I hadn't yet discovered that I am slightly nearsighted. Elisa thinks that's the reason I couldn't stand reading – because I had this eye problem, and my head got kind of dizzy when I tried to pay attention to the letters. I don't know. Maybe it was just because I never found anything interesting in books. In some books, I mean. I still find many of them incredibly boring. But that doesn't matter now. I'm not changing the subject. I'm just introducing myself.

Maybe this is the best way to begin after all, by introducing all of us. So, I'm Mariano. My father is a salesman and works for a company that sells office supplies. He is always traveling from one small town to another, showing products to stationery stores, getting new clients, that kind of thing. My mother also works a lot. Until recently she was the manager at Pastries & Savories Tea House, a kind of fancy sandwich bar in the biggest shopping center at Cachoeirinha. By the way, that's the name of our town (the official name is Cachoerinha do Rio das Pedras). But even though Cachoeirinha means little waterfall, there's just a clear creek that flows and bounces over a few rocks and ends up flowing into the Rio Pardo.

Now that's a real river. It's large, boiling (as they say in school books). Its waters are muddy because of all the earth it carries, all the way from its source, as if it has to bring along whatever is in its way to prove how important a river it is. The Rio Pardo goes through a lot of towns and farms before throwing itself into the big Rio Paraiba. These days most of the farms are dairy farms. But for a long time they were coffee plantations. That's why many of them still have huge fantastic old houses. They are part of our national heritage now, and are considered to be important. There are lots of these kinds of houses around here. Most of them are empty ruins because their owners can't afford to take care of them.

It was in one of these houses that everything happened.

My mother has a friend called Vera, who was her schoolmate and is Leo and Elisa's mother. Vera has been divorced for years and used to work as a secretary at the Cachoeirinha Dairy Farmers' Association. Every now and then she would threaten to move to a bigger city. But she stayed here to be near her parents, who lived in a small farm a little further downstream on what was left of one of those big plantations.

I was glad that she stayed, because Leo is my best friend, and I would miss him a lot if he went away. We've been in the same class since the first grade. We play soccer every weekend, usually on Feijão Field. It's named after the great soccer player from the National League, Feijão himself. Did you know that he was born in Cachoeirinha do Rio das Pedras?

He was. And he began his career playing on that field, which now has his name.

Leo and I are always together. Some people even think that we are brothers. But all you have to do is look at us to see how different we are. Milk and coffee. I'm tall and thin, and my skin is light. Leo is darker, a lot darker (not as dark as his mother and certainly not as dark as his grandmother, but dark). And he is shorter than me, but stronger. He is one year older than Elisa, who's a smart cool girl. I am not saying that just because I know that she is going to read this. I really think she is cool and smart. I always did.

From time to time, we used to spend weekends or holidays on Leo and Elisa's grandparents' farm, in that huge falling-apart house. Elisa is never a bore. Sometimes she would read by herself or play with Teresa, the granddaughter of the owners of a neighboring farm. But usually Elisa would come fishing or horseback riding with us. And she was never in our way. That's something you can't say about most girls.

Teresa, on the other hand, is very touchy. Everything bothers her. She complains that it's too hot, that the bushes are too thorny, that there are mosquitoes, that the air near the corral stinks. She won't even sit on the ground because her pants will get dirty. But you have to understand – she lives in the city and isn't used to the way things are around here, or so Elisa always says. And I have to admit that even all her complaining didn't ruin the wonderful days we spent at the farm.

When Leo's grandpa died a few months ago, my mother took me to over to Leo and Elisa's house. At first I just sat and kept my friend company. But soon – I'm ashamed to tell you this – other thoughts began to come into my mind.

One of them was that our friendship would be over soon. Dona Carlota, their grandmother, was kind of weak and not so healthy. Of course she wouldn't be able to handle all the work on the farm by herself. I realized that they would all have to live together. And it would be very easy for Vera to convince her mother to move to the city. No one had to tell me that. I could see it coming. I risked losing my perfect weekends at the farm. Much worse, I risked losing my best friend.

Some days later I talked to Leo and told him how worried I was.

"I don't know, Mariano. I don't think it will be like that," said Leo calmly.

I wasn't convinced.

"But hasn't your grandma already left the farm? Isn't she already living in town with all of you?"

"Yes, she is."

"See what I mean?" I insisted. "I don't think she'll ever go back to the farm now. Your mother is sure to move to São Paulo with the whole family."

Leo laughed. "Guess what, Mariano. It seems like my grandmother has talked my mother into living on the farm instead."

Amazing! Leo told me that the two of them had been talking a lot lately. Dona Carlota was insisting that she wanted to go back home as soon as possible. And Vera couldn't bear to sell the place where she had been born. They were trying to figure out some way to keep the farm. Vera didn't even like her job or the kind of life she was living.

But I kept worrying.

"Don't you see? Your mother is just talking like that in front of you. She keeps saying she doesn't want to go on working at the Dairy Farmers' Association to prepare you and Elisa for a move. Kind of like plowing the ground before putting in the seeds."

Leo said, "Really, Mariano, I don't think so. They aren't sure what to do. My grandpa left some money in a savings account. Not much, but some. Didn't you talk about preparing the ground? They were talking about it this morning. They said that the money is not enough to prepare the ground and grow something that could make a living."

"Didn't I tell you?"

"But they kept on talking. In the end my mother said, 'I'll just have to find a way.'"

"Do you really think she will?"

Leo's answer was not what I was expecting.

"I don't know. But Elisa has decided that she will. And you know her. When she gets an idea, she doesn't give up. That's why I'm not worried."

That evening when my mother came home from work, she said to my father, "I'm thinking of running my own business. What do you think of the idea?"

"What are you talking about?" he said, turning the TV down with the remote control, a sure sign of how disturbed he was. He is one of those people who turns the TV on and forgets about it. He doesn't watch it, but he doesn't turn it off, either. And he never turns the volume down.

"I was talking to Vera today. It was her idea. No, actually, it was Elisa's. Now I want your opinion."

They began to talk. My mother told my father that Vera had dropped by Pastries & Savories at lunchtime and said she was thinking about making some kind of living from the small farm. Vera didn't want to sell the place where she and her parents had been born. But she wasn't a farmer, didn't know how to grow anything and had very little money. Elisa had suggested opening a small country hotel or a bed-and-breakfast or an inn. The farm was on a very beautiful piece of land with woods by the creek, and boulders that formed small waterfalls on the Rio das Pedras before it threw itself into the Rio Pardo. And there were the huge ancient buildings from its days as a coffee plantation.

"What does Vera know about running hotels or inns?" my father grumped.

My mother explained that her friend was enrolling in a hotel management course. And she also explained that Vera had some money to invest in her business – her father's savings and her own, and that she could get a loan at the bank, and I don't know what else. I didn't understand much about that part.

To tell the truth, I wasn't paying attention to the

money stuff. I didn't care about the details. I could never have dreamt that all of this would lead us to a mystery. Nor that one day I would have to write about that talk in order to tell our story from the other world. I was just very excited about Elisa's idea.

But I do remember that my mother said something very important to my father that day – that Vera had asked her to be her partner. She thought maybe they could join their efforts, since my mother had some management experience, ran a tea house, and they were good friends.

My parents talked for hours that evening. I listened for a while, then I went to my room. But I could tell that my mother was very excited about her plans. And I could also tell that my father, after hearing about the plan, had decided it was interesting. He said he would help if he could. He promised to introduce them to an accountant. He said that the inn could be a good investment for some of their savings. Then he gave a deep sigh and got a dreamy look I had never seen before. He smiled and said that maybe it could be a good business for him, too, because being a salesman was very tiring. There came a time when a man needed to settle down. An inn like that could mean a way out. Things like that. I got the impression he also might want to be a partner in their business.

And that's how it all began.

Vera left her job and went to hotel school. My mother kept working at the tea house for another two months, until they found someone to replace her. But whenever they had spare time, we went to the farm with Dona Carlota.

"We must look at everything with new eyes," Vera would say. "This won't just be our house any longer. It will be a business, even if we live in a small corner of it."

The three women talked and talked. They made plans. They spent hours describing what the kitchen, the lobby and the offices would look like. They made lists of all the plumbing and electrical work that had to be done. They planned a bathroom for each bedroom. And they discussed the landscaping and the gardens, what would be kept, what had to be built or rebuilt, what could be torn down.

Leo, Elisa and I made our own suggestions — there should be a swimming pool, horses for riding, boats on the river.

They laughed. "Take it easy, kids."

"It's not as simple as that. Everything costs money."

Dona Carlota kept saying something very strange, "Bear the litter slowly, for the saint is made of clay."

After she'd said it the third time, Leo asked what

it meant. I was glad, because I didn't understand it, either. I didn't know what kind of litter she was talking about, and I couldn't see any saint nearby.

"Oh, it's an old saying about religious processions. People used to carry statues of saints down the street on their shoulders, in a little altar balanced on poles. If one person started to run, then the next one might trip, and everyone would fall down. And if the saint was made of clay or porcelain, it would break. It means be careful so that everything's in one piece when you arrive wherever you're going."

In other words because they didn't have a lot of money, they'd have to take their time.

"We need hard work, organization, dedication and, especially, lots of care. And we can only spend money on what is essential. At least during this first phase, while we're getting started," explained my mother.

After a while Vera decided they needed more bedrooms than they'd planned. She had learned at the hotel management course that an inn usually needs at least ten bedrooms to make money. That's because no matter how many bedrooms they had, they would have to pay the workers and the taxes, buy washing machines and build a proper kitchen and a whole bunch of other stuff. To pay for all that they would need a certain number of customers. So there was a whole lot more talk about finances.

The house was big, but not that big. They needed rooms for the employees and all the rooms for the
whole infra-something of the business – like a laundry room, a place for the linen, the food.

And suddenly someone said, "Maybe we could
use the shed!"

I don't even remember whose suggestion it was.

What we called the shed wasn't a real shed,
because most sheds are made of wood. This shed had
really thick walls that seemed to be built of bricks,
although I hadn't really thought much about it
before. Once the work began I found out they were
made of taipa. That's an old-fashioned type of lath-
and-plaster, if you know what that is. First, a struc-
ture was made out of straight sticks from trees, some
vertical and some horizontal, tied firmly to each
other, making a sort of net of little squares. Then the
holes in between were covered with mud and clay on
each side. When it dried, it became harder than
brick. Then all you had to do was smooth it out and
paint it.

My dad said that this was the most common con-
struction technique in Brazil until very recently,
because instead of using iron or cement, it used only
things that were at hand. It was cheap and very solid.
So solid that this shed had resisted a big fire a long
time ago, even though the roof had fallen in, as had
some parts of the walls. It was later rebuilt, although

most of the original shed had survived. But that was history, a long time in the past, long before we or even our parents and grandparents were born.

Anyway, what matters now is that this so-called shed was a very old building, long and narrow, behind the main house. It was sort of like a barn in ruins. It had no windows, and there were no inside walls. It was just one big dark room except for the light that came through a few holes in the walls and the ceiling. The floor was just earth.

The building had sometimes been used as a barn, but it had mainly been used to store all kinds of junk that Leo's grandparents didn't have the heart to throw away – an old wardrobe, a double bed that took up too much space and wasn't being used anymore, a few trunks, some chairs with straw seats that were now ripped, a couple of huge copper pans, an old pot with a hole, a pile of dishes and trays with little chipped or broken parts.

When the repairs began, Elisa even found an old candlestick made of blue and white porcelain that was broken in three parts. The breaks were so clean that she was able to glue them together into one piece. The candlestick looked as good as new, so perfect that you could even read the inscription on the bottom – Freewood – the name of the factory where it had been made.

The shed could have been a great place to play,

but we didn't really like going there. It was too dark and lugubrious. (Did you like that? I learned that word in a book Elisa lent me and thought I'd never get a chance to use it. If you don't like it, you could choose another. *Gloomy*, *dismal* or *mournful* would do, too.) When the wind came in through the holes in the wall, it sounded like a pack of wolves howling in a horror movie. Every time the door opened a bat would fly out. And there were also some strange noises that Elisa swore were mice.

Anyway, this ruined shed was a thing of the past. Nobody really remembered what it had been like just a short while ago, because after the work began on it, Vera started to call it the "annex." And with the building of the annex, the inn began to look the way it does today. And that is why so many tourists from São Paulo now come to stay.

2

SOMEONE CRYING IN
THE NIGHT

You can imagine our excitement when we kids were finally able to use the annex before the official opening of the inn. There were still no guests, and we were going to be the very first people to sleep there. The electricity hadn't even been turned on yet. But the rooms had been built – they had walls, floors, windows and were painted, although there wasn't any furniture. The carpenter was late delivering the beds and nightstands.

Almost all the work at the inn had fallen behind schedule. But nobody was as late as the carpenters. The roof, windows, doors and even the chicken pen were still missing. My mother wanted the inn to have a chicken yard with a little wooden fence around it because people from the city love to see animals when they come to the countryside, and there are children who think eggs are born at the supermarket. And Vera and her mother also thought it would be good to have chickens and other birds. ("With animals in the yard we can always have a back-up for dinner in case of an emergency," said Dona Carlota.)

But the poultry farm delivered the birds before the pen was built. So there we were with chickens, ducks and even guinea fowls behind such a rickety fence that they kept escaping, and we had to chase them around the yard.

"Hey! Catch that chicken!"

"There goes the duck."

"Run, the hen's getting away!"

I think the first thing I learned at the inn was to recognize poultry. There was the chick with the bare neck, the little rooster who picked fights with all the others, a few red hens and a few white ones, and the big *carijó* rooster and chickens with their white-and-black speckled feathers. And there was the guinea fowl that was the same color as the *carijó* but a different shape with light fluffy feathers. It crowed a different way.

Whatever kind of bird, they were all a lot of trouble, so much trouble that everyone kept begging the carpenter to finish the fence and the chicken coop. This meant that the beds weren't delivered on time.

And so on the day the inn was supposed to open,

all the poultry were very comfortable, but people couldn't check in. There was no furniture.

But since the basic building was ready, my mother and Vera agreed to let us children spend the night. They told us a thousand times not to get anything dirty. We were allowed to use the new mattresses on the floor. But there were a thousand and one conditions. They told us they were not going to hang the paintings on the walls (as if we cared), and that they weren't going to let us use the new sheets, blankets, pillowcases and towels. Those things would be saved until the inn was completely ready. So we had to bring our own linen.

We asked a few friends to spend the first night in the annex with us. At the last minute my parents decided to join us. We piled into three bedrooms – the girls in one, the boys in another and my parents in the third.

We went to bed late because we stayed on the porch talking and playing the guitar for quite a while. But we had had a very full day with horseback riding and swimming in the river. We were all exhausted. When we finally decided to go to sleep, we lay down on the beds – or the mattresses, to be exact – and passed out.

I don't really know how long I had been there when I woke up. It was so dark, I couldn't see a thing.

But I could hear. There was a noise. It wasn't very clear, but I recognized the sound of moaning and sobbing. Someone was crying. And it was such sad sobbing, it broke my heart, even though it was muffled. I couldn't make out where it was coming from. I figured it must be in the girls' room since it wasn't that close to me, and I was sure no boy would cry like that in the middle of the night.

I lifted my head, sat up and listened carefully for some time. Yes, there was definitely someone crying and not too close by. I decided to wake Leo, who was lying next to me.

"Leo, wake up!" I whispered.

"What is it? Is everything okay?" he asked, his voice sounding startled and loud in the darkness.

"I think someone might be sick."

"Who? What happened? Did anyone call us?" he asked loudly.

"Will you two stop talking? I want to sleep!" groaned a sleepy voice.

I tried to explain in a low whisper. "There's someone crying, and I think it's coming from the girls' bedroom."

He went quiet. After a while I thought he must have fallen asleep again. Then he said, "I can't hear anything except crickets, frogs and the wind in the leaves."

It was true. The crying had stopped. Even I couldn't hear it anymore.

"It must have been a dream," said Leo.

In the darkness I could hear my friend turning over on the mattress. And then total silence. He had probably gone back to sleep. But I couldn't. I was absolutely sure I hadn't dreamt it. And the crying girl had managed to wake me up completely.

I turned on the flashlight, went out into the hallway and walked back and forth. I stopped in front of the girls' room. I figured that if the crying person needed help, she would see the light from under the door and could come out and talk. But nobody did. Whoever it was, she had probably let all her sadness out and was sleeping again.

I went back to bed and closed my eyes. But I was quite worried. (I remember how I felt as if it were only yesterday.) It took a while before I fell asleep again, but not before the roosters had crowed several times, and the sun was rising.

I was the last one to wake up. When I went to have breakfast, everybody else had finished. I was a little embarrassed. I just drank a mug of milk quickly, grabbed a piece of bread with butter and ran out to meet the others. They were already in the orchard, climbing guava trees.

I checked out all the girls carefully, trying to figure out which one had been crying the night before in such a sad way. None of them looked at all tired or upset. Apparently the girl who had been crying was pretty good at hiding it.

But at the end of the day I got a surprise. We were lying around on the porch talking. Suddenly someone said, "Let's scare Elisa!"

I saw that she had fallen asleep, lying in the hammock. We all gathered around her laughing and shouting.

"Isn't it a bit early to be sleeping, Elisa?"

And Leo said, "What is it, are you going to bed with the chickens now, like Grandma says?"

Elisa laughed. But then she said, "Don't worry, I don't usually fall asleep this early. It's just that I slept really badly last night. I was up for hours."

"What happened? Was the mattress uncomfort-able?" someone asked.

"No," she answered vaguely. "I guess I'm just not used to the annex and all its different noises."

So she was the one. People were already changing the subject, but I was curious. I sat down next to her and said, "I was up during the night, too, Elisa. And it took me a long time to get back to sleep, too."

I wondered whether I should ask her why she had been crying, but I hesitated. I didn't want to seem too nosy. I thought it was better to give her a chance to speak up if she wanted to.

She looked at me very seriously. She paused for a moment, then asked, "So you saw it and heard it, too?"

"Saw what?"

"A light wandering around the floor," she answered, so low I could hardly hear her.

"That was me, Elisa, with the flashlight, walking around the hall."

"Why didn't you call me?"

"How was I supposed to know you were awake?"

"Well, it was a bit hard to sleep with you crying like that. What was wrong? Were you sick?"

"No," I protested immediately. "I wasn't crying! But the sobbing and moaning woke me up, too. I even talked to Leo about it, but by then the crying had stopped, and we couldn't hear anything else."

She looked at me as though she didn't really believe me. Then she must have made a decision, because she said, "Mariano, if it wasn't you, and it wasn't me who was crying, then who was it? Because I'm sure I heard crying, very clearly. Someone was sobbing."

"And moaning," I added. "I heard it, too. It must have been one of the other girls."

She denied it.

"No, Mariano, it wasn't. It didn't come from our room. I had the candlestick and a box of matches next to my mattress. I lit the candle to see if it was any of the girls, but it wasn't. I'm sure of it. They were all asleep. And the sound was a bit muffled. Though it seemed to get louder once I lit the candle. It sounded like it came from far away."

The crying hadn't come from the boy's room. I was sure of that, too. Could it have been my mother? But I didn't know why she would be crying like that in the middle of the night. I was worried, but I tried not to show it.

"It was probably just someone having a bad dream. We'll find out later."

We hadn't solved the mystery. At least not that day.

If I had more practice writing, I could probably come up with a lie like: we spent days and days wondering about the crying in the dark. I think it would help increase the suspense. But it's not true. By the next weekend we had pretty much forgotten all about it.

For a few days I had checked out my mother's face without her noticing what I was doing. I was trying to find out whether she looked sad or tear-stained, however that would look. But I couldn't see a thing. In fact, she had never seemed so excited, what with all the preparations for the inn's official opening and the beginning of her own business. I finally had to admit that she couldn't have been the one crying that night.

To tell you the truth, I started to think that there hadn't been anyone crying. Elisa and I had probably just been scared by one of those sounds you hear in places you're not used to. A tree branch brushing against the wall in the wind, maybe. Or a window that hadn't been shut properly making screeching sounds. Or a stray cat or an owl or some other night bird. Who knows?

I became sure that was it. After a while we no longer thought about the sobbing and moaning in the night.

That is, until it started up again, on another night. And the crying wasn't all that started up this time.

3

CLEAR
AND TRANSPARENT

IT HAPPENED almost a month later. By then everything was ready. The electricity was on, and guests were starting to show up for a weekend at the inn. We could no longer gather all our friends to sleep over in a room on mattresses. Now there were beds, desks, televisions, carpets, curtains, mirrors and lamps in every room. There were even prints on the walls, reproductions of some old drawings by some guy named Rugendas and another guy called Debret. My mother had ordered the pictures from São Paulo.

"It helps to recreate the atmosphere of the old days," she said.

She explained that these artists, one German and the other French, had traveled throughout Brazil at the beginning of the nineteenth century.

They painted everything in sight to show the world what we were like. Now years later Brazilians can also see what we were like back then – the landscapes, the houses, the native people, the slaves, the masters, the furniture, the kinds of jobs people had, what they used to wear, the traveling scientists, lots of things. Everything the way it used to be in the old days. They are cool to look at. It's all recorded for ever, even though there was no photography at the time.

The prints that my mother had ordered were different from one another, so we ended up naming the rooms after them. It was a way to tell the rooms apart since the furniture, the sheets and the curtains were all the same, especially in the annex, where all the rooms were new and about the same size. In the main house the rooms were different – some bigger, some smaller, with windows that opened onto different parts of the yard.

Since there were still very few guests at the inn, our mothers would let us stay in a couple of bedrooms on the weekends even if we couldn't bring the whole gang. They said that we helped give a feeling of "movement" in the inn so that the guests wouldn't feel as if they were all alone. We asked Tere to keep Elisa company. Leo and Elisa would come over from the little apartment at the back of the inn, where

they were living, and I would trade Cachoeirinha for the annex.

Elisa and Tere alternated between the Banana Leaf Saleswoman room and the Naturalist's room — the one with the drawing of a man followed by a slave in a big hat with a bunch of butterflies pinned to it, carrying drawings, files, samples of flowers and leaves and a dead snake on the tip of a stick.

Leo and I would stay in the room next door, the one with the Flowers and Coconut Salesman, or in the Hunter, with the print of a really strong native man lying on his back, holding a huge bow with his feet, getting ready to shoot an arrow. Those were the four rooms that were still kind of incomplete, because the seamstress was late with the delivery of the curtains that would match the sheets.

Well, on this night and in this place came what you might call the second chapter of "the crying in the night." That is, if it really can be described as crying.

Only this time it happened a lot earlier. We weren't even asleep yet. I mean, the rest of the people staying at the inn were probably dreaming by then, considering when they went to bed. But the four of us had stayed up putting together a five-hundred-piece jigsaw puzzle in the Banana Leaf Saleswoman room – that is to say, the girls' room. It was one of those puzzles that was the perfect level of difficulty – not hard enough to make you give up, nor easy enough to be a bore. We got carried away and didn't even notice time pass.

It was Friday night. During the afternoon when we arrived, we had set out all the pieces that had one straight side and had completed the outline of the puzzle. Afterwards we had gathered the most obvious pieces and put them together, so we could already imagine the whole thing. We thought we could finish it that same night, so we kept on talking and putting the puzzle together until it was quite late.

It's always harder to work at night, because electric light isn't as good as daylight, and sometimes the colors get a little mixed up. But there were lots of us, and that helped. When one of us couldn't figure something out, another could.

"Try this one, Elisa. I think it's the same dark green as that one, from that tree you were putting together!"

"Yeah, it looks like it. Let me see."

I handed her the piece. One, two tries. "I don't think it fits," she said.

"Try turning it the other way around," I suggested.

"Like this?"

"It fits!"

"One more!" celebrated Leo.

"Or one less. Hey, maybe we can finish tonight."

Suddenly Tere stood up. She seemed to be listening. Then she asked, "Do you guys hear any weird noises?"

"It's only the wind, silly," answered Leo impatiently. "You're always getting scared for nothing. What's the matter? Doesn't the wind ever blow at your grandfather's farm?"

Elisa answered for her, "Of course it does. But she doesn't live there, remember? She only goes for the weekend. And not even all weekends. She's not used to it like we are. The wind probably doesn't blow as hard in the city."

"The wind is the same everywhere," I said.

"The wind might be the same, but in the countryside there are more trees, the houses are older and smaller, the sounds might be different," argued Elisa, defending her friend.

"I've never heard anything about the size of a house changing the sound of the wind. The problem is that the two of you..." Leo started to say, but all of a sudden he was interrupted by a different sound, one that we all heard. One that we couldn't deny.

"Did you hear it this time?" asked Tere.

All you had to do was look at our faces to see that we had, and that it was very strange. Elisa opened her eyes wide and grabbed my arm. Leo put his finger over his mouth asking for silence.

We were quiet. I don't know for how long. But we didn't hear any more.

"It sounded like someone moving furniture. But where?" I said, just to say something and to try to get rid of that little feeling of fear you get after being startled.

"Right. It may be. But only if it's metal," said Elisa,

reminding us of what we had all heard very clearly.

"Or some heavy chains being dragged," added Tere, almost in a whisper. "Like in ghost movies."

"It must have been a sound from one of the pipes. The hot water running through them sometimes makes weird noises."

"Yeah, that's right!" I agreed. "Tere isn't used to this system of water heating. It does make a lot of noise sometimes."

We were all familiar with that. A lot of the old houses used this kind of water heating. I went on explaining, "There are pipes that carry the water by the wood stove to get heated, and then they go around the rest of the house, and then…"

"But… we don't have a wood stove here, and all the heating is done by gas," interrupted Elisa.

"Then it was the wind," insisted Leo. "It's very windy tonight."

It really was. It looked like it would soon be storming. Every now and then we could hear thunder far away, but it seemed to be getting closer all the time.

We looked out the window. There were no stars in the sky. It must have been really cloudy. There was some lightning around the Pedra Negra mountain.

Suddenly we heard the sound again. It was inside the house, no doubt about it.

"It must be the thunder echoing," said Leo, not sounding too convinced.

"Yeah. That's probably right," I said, trying to support my friend.

At that moment Elisa said something amazing. "Of course it wasn't thunder. And it was right here, in the annex. We all heard it perfectly. Let's stop being silly trying to come up with explanations and go find out what it is!"

We boys couldn't let a girl take action like that, all alone.

"Let's go," said Leo and I.

But Tere didn't seem too thrilled with the idea.

"Actually, I don't really want to go. Can't one of you stay here with me?"

"Either we all go, or nobody goes," decided Elisa, who seemed to be taking charge of the situation.

"Okay, so we'll stay," said Leo, "and if we hear the sound again, we'll all go."

Before anyone could answer, a strong burst of wind blew, and as often happens in Cachoeirinha, the lights suddenly went out.

"Great! That's just what we needed!" I complained.

"I'm scared," moaned Tere.

"This always happens," Leo said, trying to calm her down. "A tree branch probably fell on a wire.

The emergency people from the electric company will be here soon to fix it."

I doubted it. "At this time of night?"

"Did you bring your flashlight?" asked Elisa.

It was really dark, but I knew the question was meant for me.

"I didn't think we were going to need it," I answered.

"It's okay. I have a candle and some matches on my candlestick over there on the desk."

In a moment we saw the light from a match, but it went out so fast that it didn't even get close to the candle. In the darkness Elisa's voice creaked, "These match factories are getting worse and worse. They keep using bad wood. If you strike the match at all hard, it breaks."

She tried again. The same thing happened. At the third strike, the light grew stronger. A flash of lightning lit up the room at the same time. I thought I saw someone standing by the door, but I wasn't sure. It got dark again too quickly. I kept looking over in that direction.

Before Elisa struck the fourth match, I heard Tere's trembling voice. "It's so windy that the curtain has come down. It blew over there by the door."

I remembered that this room didn't have curtains yet. But I didn't have time to say anything.

Elisa managed to light the candle. Then we all saw.

Standing next to the door wearing a long white dress and a turban on her head, black skinned and barefoot as if she'd just come out of one of Debret's drawings, stood a girl about our age.

Perfectly clear. But kind of transparent.

4

A STRANGE CONVERSATION

No one said a word. Then all of a sudden we all spoke at the same time.

"Who are you?"

"How did you get in here?"

"Oh, my God!"

"What are you doing in my bedroom?"

The girl didn't answer. She didn't even move. But she stared at us, wide-eyed, examining us one by one as if she wanted to know all about us just by looking.

Elisa squeezed my arm so hard it almost hurt. But she seemed in complete control when she asked as cool as always, "Is there a problem? Can we help?"

If someone had just come in and heard the question, he might have thought Elisa was speaking to the daughter of a guest, who had strayed from her room in the middle of the storm. But such a girl wouldn't have been transparent nor wearing a long white outfit like a *baiana* or *mucama*'s carnival costume.

The girl neither moved nor spoke. She stared. She might even have been shaking a little.

I must confess I was a little bit scared myself. Not too scared though, because I thought I didn't believe in ghosts. And because I knew I wasn't alone. My friends were there with me, and there were other people sleeping nearby, behind the doors along that same corridor. But looking at that strange girl standing there, completely transparent, and being able to see the door behind her, even in the faint candlelight, would scare anyone. I think the reason why I wasn't more afraid is because the girl wasn't at all threatening. On the contrary, I thought she seemed terrified, a lot more so than the four of us put together.

Elisa must have felt the same because she said, "Don't be afraid. Nobody is going to hurt you."

The girl nodded. Then Elisa introduced everyone as if she were at a party.

"My name is Elisa, this is my brother Leo, this is our friend Mariano. And the girl over there is Teresa. We call her Tere. How about you? What's your name?"

The answer came in such a faint whisper, we weren't even sure we'd heard it.

"Rosario."

"Rosalia?" repeated Leo.

"No. Maria do Rosario."

So the ghost could talk. She could talk normally. That made us feel more at ease. I was even comfortable enough to try to continue the conversation.

"And how did you get here?"

The girl's answer was as clear and transparent as she was. "I live here."

"Here?" the four of us asked so loudly that she fell silent and didn't say any more.

For a few moments the room was quiet. We looked at Rosario, she looked at us, but nobody said a word.

Then Leo, always looking for a rational explanation, had the idea that she might be the daughter of one of the guests.

"Are your parents spending the weekend here?"

"No."

And that was it. No further explanations. But we felt calmer. As for me, I can remember being more curious than scared. Rosario was a girl like us, she was answering our questions, and we couldn't even see through her anymore. I was starting to think that the seeing-through thing was just because we were frightened and there was candlelight – some kind of optical illusion.

But I still thought Elisa went a bit overboard. Feeling all friendly, she reached out her hand to the girl and said, "Don't just stand there. Come and join us. We were putting together a jigsaw puzzle, but then the lights went out. But we can talk until they come back on. Here, you can sit on my bed."

While Elisa talked, the other girl stared as if she didn't understand a word. But she did get the last part, the invitation to come closer. She didn't give Elisa her hand, but she took a little step forward. Tere moved back and stood a little further away. As if in a slow-motion dance, we all moved until we were sitting down, except for Rosario. But finally when Elisa insisted, she sat on the edge of the bed.

She looked around the room but didn't say a word. Then she smiled and pointed, "Iaia's candlestick!"

"I found it in the shed and thought it was pretty," Elisa answered, as if it were the most ordinary thing to do in the world. "It was broken, but I found all the pieces. There were just a few of them, and they were big. So I glued them back together. I didn't know the candlestick belonged to anyone. But if you want, you can take it and give it back to Iaia. I don't want to keep it if it belongs to someone else."

"You can keep it. Iaia gave it to me. Now it's yours. I don't need it."

That was a lot of information all of a sudden. Almost a speech, or a story. Until then Rosario had hardly said a word. We had no idea at that point of all the things she would tell us later. We were curious and excited.

Even Tere felt brave enough to ask, "Who is Iaia? Is she your sister?"

The expression on the girl's face changed, as if she

were hiding a smile. "Sister! Don't even say such a thing. Iaia is the lady of the house. The good one. The master's daughter. He's the bad one. And the mistress, her mother, is…"

We never found out what Rosario was going to say. Because at that exact moment, we heard a *cock-a-doodle-doo*! coming from the chicken yard. The girl who was just starting to feel at ease talking to us in our bedroom stopped in the middle of a sentence and began to look transparent, the way she had at the beginning of our meeting.

"The *carijó* rooster!" she said.

And she began to fade away, right before our eyes, as if she were a cloud of smoke being scattered by the wind.

Elisa tried to object. "Hey! What's going on? You're leaving, just like that, right in the middle of our conversation? And without even saying good-bye? That's not very polite, you know!"

But Rosario was fading quickly. She was only there for a few more seconds, her voice growing fainter and fainter. "Call me again, and I'll come back," she said.

We tried. We kept saying her name out loud. We called so much that we woke up a guest who shouted to complain about the noise. My mother came and told us off and sent us to bed immediately.

But Rosario didn't return.

5

BLACK PIECES, WHITE DOTS

OF COURSE we hardly slept that night, because with all that had happened, time passed without us noticing. The roosters were beginning to crow. Day was coming.

Leo and I had gone to our room, and the girls had stayed in theirs. But what kept us from sleeping wasn't the storm. It was the memory of the events of that night. We talked for ages, going over the strange encounter and trying to understand what had happened.

We had never been up so early for breakfast. We were dying to be able to go somewhere where no one would listen, where we could talk in peace. We wanted to go outside and be alone, but it was raining, and we had to stay indoors. That meant we had to help our mothers with the chores, because at the inn there was always work to do.

But finally the rain stopped. As soon as we could, we gathered at the riverbank and sat on a big stone. It had a kind of bench-like platform at the back under a huge tree. It was still quite wet, but at least it was a place where nobody would bother us. So we started to go over our night's adventure.

We argued a lot, especially about whether Rosario was really a ghost. Leo had strong opinions.

"She can't be. There's no such thing as ghosts."

"But she was transparent," Tere reminded us.

"Only at first, when we were looking at her from a certain angle. But maybe that was just an illusion.

Afterwards when she sat on Elisa's bed, she talked normally, just like one of us."

"So how come she disappeared all of a sudden?"

"Maybe she had to be home early and was afraid her mother would tell her off."

"And so she faded away?" insisted Tere. "As if she were drying up, like a puddle evaporating in the heat after it rains?"

"I don't know, it was so dark. Maybe we couldn't see properly."

"What about the sounds we heard?" I asked.

"Well, that might have been..."

Before we could continue, Elisa interrupted. "You know what I think? None of this matters. She may have been a ghost, a spirit from the afterlife, a being from another planet or a mass hallucination. It doesn't make any difference. Ghost or no ghost, we all saw her, we all talked to her. And we all want to meet Rosario again, right?"

"If she's a ghost, I'm not so happy about it," confessed Tere.

"Well, I do, anyway. If she's not a ghost, she can be our friend. And if she is, she must have had a pretty strong reason to show up here. We have to help her."

"Well, that's true," I agreed.

In the end we decided to try to call Rosario again.

But we didn't know if it would work because when we'd tried last night, she hadn't shown up.

Before bed we gathered in the girls' room. We stared at the Debret picture on the wall.

"If that slave girl's skirt wasn't blue, and if it wasn't so puffy, it would be just like Rosario's," said Tere, who always paid attention to fashion. She examined the print and the slave girl's clothes. "Even the handkerchief on her head is similar. And the scarf over her shoulder."

It was true. The outfits did look alike.

"Maybe they bought their clothes in the same store," suggested Leo, who was always teasing Tere.

"For God's sake, Leo, don't start," complained Elisa. "If we really want to find a way to call Rosario back, we have to concentrate, not make jokes."

But it didn't work, no matter how hard we concentrated. We tried calling her over and over, but she didn't come.

It reminded me of a concert where the singer asks the audience to sing with him, and the audience stays quiet.

We said her name all together, as loud as we could without waking the guests. Then we repeated it softly, in a whisper, as if it were a secret or a prayer. But nothing.

Then just the girls called.

Nothing.

Just Leo and I.

Nothing.

One by one.

Nothing.

Either she was deaf, or she came only when she wanted to. Or maybe we needed to call her in some special way, and we weren't getting it right.

"There has to be a way, but we don't know it yet. There's got to be a key to open the passage," insisted Elisa.

"A kind of password to another dimension? Interesting," said Leo. "It makes sense."

"Passage?" I said, not understanding or maybe not wanting to. "I don't get it. To where?"

"How should I know? To another world, I guess."

"Oh, my God!" exclaimed Tere.

If there really was a passage, we couldn't find it, no matter how hard we tried. Elisa remembered that we had heard someone crying on that first night in the annex. We told Leo and Tere about what had happened, and they were amazed and kind of upset that we hadn't told them about it before. We even exaggerated a little to make it more exciting. We mentioned voices, cries for help.

But thinking about these appearances, we finally realized that in both cases, the meeting with Rosario (that is, if we could describe hearing sobbing as a meeting), hadn't happened because of anything we had done. We had to admit that while we could be visited by her, we didn't seem to be able to invite her back. As for going there – where? – to pay her a visit, that was impossible. Obviously none of us wanted to leave our world or dimension, even just for a while, even if we could. That wasn't an option. Besides that, we considered every other possible thing we might do. We talked and talked, but no one had any bright ideas.

When the weekend was over, we separated. But we had reached one conclusion and arrived at two possible courses of action.

The conclusion – despite it being a lot harder than we thought, we wanted to keep trying to reach Rosario. The first possible action – next Friday we would meet again in the Banana Leaf Saleswoman room. The second – during the week we would do research into anything that could possibly work in our situation.

Tere and I, who lived in cities, would look in libraries. "Check out the Internet, Mariano, don't forget!" reminded Tere, who was nervous about some country stuff but was very good at computers and technology.

Leo and Elisa now lived full time at the inn. They

took the bus to Cachoeirinha every day to go to school but had to come right back. So they didn't have as much time for research as we did. And since there was only one phone line at their grandparents' old house, and there wasn't a high-speed connection yet, they couldn't surf the web. Vera insisted that the phone be free at all times. But they said they would try to find out anything they could.

On Friday when we were finally alone, we talked about what we had learned. Tere spoke out right away. She said she was not going to take part in any rituals to call back the souls of dead people. It sounded like she had spent the whole week rehearsing her speech.

"From my research I have discovered that there have been many events of this kind, although in general, spirits manifest themselves independently from the will of the living," she said.

We looked at her as though she were the ghost. But I think Tere had memorized what she wanted to say, because she went on as if she were reciting from a book.

"On many an occasion, however, and often for religious reasons, there have been episodes where the living have taken on the task of communicating with the afterlife and invoking the spirits of the dead. For my part, I would like to make it quite clear that I reject this possibility completely. I have no intention of participating in such a ceremony and ask that you respect my decision."

Then she sighed and added in a more normal tone of voice and using everyday words, "Please, you guys, I looked all this up because we agreed to, and you're my friends, and I love you. I spent all week reading stories about ouija boards and seances, and I got information on shamans from primitive tribes who get in touch with the other world. But I don't like any of this stuff at all. If you really want to go ahead, that's okay. But I would prefer that you did it sometime when I'm not sleeping over."

I said that I understood. I respected Tere, and if she felt that way, we had no right to push her into doing something she didn't want to do. I admired her courage in saying how she felt so firmly. Because I must admit, I wasn't all that comfortable with the idea, either. I was feeling quite divided. On the one hand, I wasn't very keen on all this, but on the other, I was tempted by my curiosity.

The other two reacted very differently from me.

"Come on, Tere, cut it out," said Leo. "We all agreed to do this. You can't turn back now. And don't think you can fool me using all those long words. You're just scared!"

"Yes, I am," said Tere. "And I'm not afraid to

admit it. I'm not trying to fool anyone – you guys say you're my friends."

"We are your friends, Tere, you know that," assured Elisa. "And if you don't want to be part of it, that's okay. I think it's silly, but we can talk about that another time. Meanwhile I promise that I won't do anything you don't want me to."

Silence.

But Elisa's promise helped clear the air. The unpleasant feeling that we were about to have a fight went away.

Feeling better, Tere went on with the conversation. "What about you, Mariano?" she asked. "Did you find out anything?"

"Well," I answered. "My line of work was less technical, so to speak. I didn't investigate the way of, let's say, obtaining this communication. I focused mainly on the fictional accounts, that is, stories that writers have invented or told about the subject."

"Oh, it's a contagious disease! Now he thinks he has to use big words, too," teased Leo. "Stop talking like that, Mariano, and admit that you spent the whole week reading ghost stories and horror comics and watching scary videos."

"Yeah, okay," I agreed, relieved that I could talk normally again. Even I didn't know why I was imitating Tere and expressing myself that way. "I found out lots of interesting things. For example, if Rosario really is a ghost and appeared here, before our eyes, it's because there is something important to her about this place or about us. Something isn't letting her rest in peace. And she will keep wanting to come back until it's settled. And there's more. If she came because she wants to or needs to, it will be very difficult for us to get her back just because we want to. Our will isn't enough. We're not that powerful."

"But she did tell us to call her back after all," Elisa reminded us.

I took a deep breath.

"So, in that case, if we make things the same as they were when she came before, it might work."

"Now that makes sense! It seems scientific – the principle of cause and effect. The same causes create the same effects. But what exactly would making it the same be?" asked Leo.

"That's what we have to figure out," I answered.

"If Tere is willing, and my little sister lets us," he said.

"That's okay. I can live with that," said Tere, which kind of surprised me. "I just don't want to be part of ceremonies I don't understand. But to do what we did that night – that's our normal life. When she showed up, we were hanging out as usual, having fun, talking, not doing anything weird. I don't mind doing that again."

It was my turn to ask. "How about you two? Did you find out anything?"

"I think I found out who Iaia is," answered Elisa. "I asked my grandmother, and she said she had heard the name before. There was a Dona Iaia who lived here many, many years ago, when her grandfather was alive."

"Our great-great-grandfather," explained Leo.

"And was this Iaia part of your family?"

"I wondered the same thing, but my grandmother said no. She was one of the former owners of the farm, which was much bigger back then and didn't belong to us, by the way. And there's more. You won't believe it. My grandmother said it was good that I asked, because this Dona Iaia was someone very important to all of us, and it's about time we heard her story."

"What story?"

"When I asked her to tell me, she said it was a very long story, and she was too busy. I insisted, and she finally promised that she would tell us on the weekend, when we were all together."

"Then it's settled!" said Tere. "Tomorrow we'll ask Dona Carlota to tell us the whole thing."

"I also found out some interesting stuff," said

Leo, "the main thing being that the annex used to be the *senzala*, the slave quarters."

"What?"

"That's right. This very place where we're sitting was the *senzala*, where the slaves used to sleep in the old days when this place was a huge rich powerful coffee farm. It was one of the biggest in the region."

I think it took me a while to make sense of all this, because I asked a stupid question.

"Does that mean your family used to be rich?"

Elisa answered, "Aren't you paying attention, Mariano? Didn't you hear what I just said? Back then the farm belonged to Iaia's family, not ours."

"But if you bought it from them, you must have had a lot of money. Not just anyone can buy a farm like that out of the blue."

"If we did, we must have lost it all," interrupted Leo impatiently. "There's no trace of it left. Now can we put my family finances aside and get back to the subject?"

"Sure," I agreed, a bit awkwardly.

Elisa continued, "Well, if we think about all of this, maybe we can put it together."

"Like a jigsaw puzzle," remembered Tere.

"Or dominoes," I said.

They looked at me blankly. I tried to explain.

"Sorry, it's just something that came into my

mind. Yesterday when I was leaving the library, I saw some old men playing dominoes in the park. I stopped and stared at all those little black pieces with their little white dots and started thinking that dominoes are like a puzzle, only easier. Instead of putting the pieces together by their shape, they are connected by the number of dots. But it's the same idea. As simple as that."

6

IAIA'S CANDLESTICK

THEY STARED at me as if I were completely crazy, going on about dominoes, which had nothing to do with the subject. Maybe they didn't. Or maybe I wasn't being clear. I felt stupid, and I didn't say any more.

Then Elisa said, "It's okay, Mariano, I get it. Then let's put the pieces of the puzzle together or play dominoes. First piece – Rosario said she lived here. Second – Leo has found out that this used to be the *senzala*."

"And I found out that Rosario's outfit looked like the one on the slave girl in the drawing, which means that she is probably a slave," said Tere.

"Is or was?"

"What's the difference?"

"Well, if she *is*, then it's because she's alive and there's still slavery. If she *was*, it's because she lived a long time ago, and she's a ghost," insisted Leo with his usual logic. "In that case Tere can't avoid the fact."

"Okay, Leo," said Elisa. "We think Rosario is a spirit or the ghost of a slave who lived in this *senzala* a long time ago. But we still want to communicate with her. Do we all? You, too? Or are you still claiming you don't believe in ghosts?"

The silence was answer enough.

Elisa went on. "This Iaia must have been the slave master's daughter. He was a bad man. But she must have been good, or Rosario's friend, because she gave her the candlestick. Right?"

"Right," I agreed.

"And according to Mariano's theory, if we want to meet her again, we'll have to do what we were doing the first time, right?" said Leo.

"Right," I repeated.

"But what were we doing? Do we have to wait for a thunderstorm and be putting together the puzzle on the table? And hope that the lights go out?"

"Maybe, Tere. We'll have to try it."

Suddenly I had an idea. I discovered another missing piece.

"Maybe we don't need the lightning. Maybe turning off the lights would be enough."

"Then let's find out," said Leo and switched off the lights.

We sat in the dark waiting for something to happen. We called Rosario's name, but nothing happened. We heard some weird metallic noises, a bit like water passing through pipes. And there was some moaning far away. But we couldn't tell whether it was an owl or someone crying.

I felt a chill go down my spine. As much as I wanted to solve the mystery, I wasn't so sure this was the way to do it.

"Did we leave the window open? Suddenly I'm feeling cold," said Tere.

"That's called goose bumps," said Leo's voice. "It's a sign of fear."

"Stop teasing, Leo!" said Elisa.

"It's okay, Elisa, he's right. I am scared. I think the hairs on my arms are standing up," whispered Tere.

"And I can hear your teeth rattling and your knees knocking together."

We all heard something. But it didn't seem to be coming from Tere.

After a while she said, "Can't you light the candle, Elisa? So we can at least see whose teeth are rattling, because I know it's not me."

"Of course, that's it! Now I get it!" cried Elisa. "That must be the missing piece. We have to light Iaia's candlestick. Last time Rosario showed up in the candlelight."

"You're probably right," I said excitedly. "Come to think of it, the other night when we heard crying, I came through the corridor with the flashlight, and you said you lit the candle in the candlestick, didn't you?"

"Yes!" agreed Elisa. "Well remembered, Mariano. There must be some connection."

"Especially now that we know the candlestick belonged to her," I continued. "It's probably been here all along. It must have been the only kind of light they had in the *senzala*."

"No," said Leo. "They must have had other stuff – fires, oil lamps, candles in bottles. This candlestick is made of English china. It's really delicate, imported from abroad. It probably wasn't used in the slave quarters."

"But we know that it belonged to Rosario after Iaia gave it to her."

"Of course, Tere. All I'm saying is that in general, the lighting in here must have been different."

"But the effect was probably the same. The kind of light this candle gives must be a lot like what they used to have in the *senzala* during slavery times," I said. "I mean, we're not just copying what we did that night. In a way, we're also making a bridge to the time when Rosario lived."

The discussion didn't go any further because at that moment Elisa struck a match, which went right out. We were all quiet. The noises had stopped. The second match lit the candle. The flame flickered a little but soon steadied. There was quite a lot of light. Nobody's teeth were chattering, and no one was making any noise.

Outside in the corridor we heard sounds we didn't recognize. But then they stopped.

The door squeaked and opened a little.

Slowly, in came Rosario. She was sliding, as if her bare feet were skating along the floor. But she didn't walk through the wall or appear out of nowhere. She came through the door like a normal person. She wasn't even transparent. The only thing that showed she wasn't normal was just a little thing, a small detail, very small indeed.

Rosario had no shadow. I remember noticing this very clearly and telling myself that I didn't need to have goose bumps. This wasn't important. Peter Pan didn't have a shadow, either, and he was a good guy. But I couldn't take my eyes off the wall, as if I were staring at a movie on a big screen. The light from the candle cast shadows from all four of us. But it went right through Rosario. Oh, well, nobody's perfect.

At least this time she wasn't quiet or looking scared. She spoke right out.

"Good evening!"

We answered all at once and started to talk.

7

BLACK BEANS
AND RICE

"MY LORD, it took you so long! I thought you were never going to find a way to call me back."

"Take it easy, Rosario. We didn't know what to do. You didn't explain how to do it. That's why we took so long. You don't have to get impatient," explained Elisa.

"I'm sure you wouldn't be so patient if you were in my place. I've lost count of how many years I have spent wandering through these burnt walls, whistling and trying to call somebody. But I could only try at night, and nobody slept here. A long time ago when some men came to fix the walls and make this roof, I thought I had a chance. But they left before dark. And I kept calling, but there was no one to hear. I wonder if you'd be patient after so much waiting, thinking that you'd finally be able to talk to someone, and then having them disappear?"

"I'm sorry, Rosario, but you're the one who disappeared. And so suddenly," said Tere. It was the first time she had spoken to Rosario directly.

"It was because of the rooster. Especially the *carijó*. After the *carijó* crows to announce the dawn, I have to leave. Do you think it's easy going back and forth all the time? Just like going for a walk, just as if I were going to fetch water at the fountain with a jug on my head?"

"What's that about your head? What happened? Did you bump your head on something?" asked Tere, who really didn't know much about country things.

"A jug, a big pitcher, silly, to carry water in," explained Elisa impatiently. "Don't interrupt. We know we haven't got long. The rooster might crow, and Rosario will have to leave again."

But time wasn't so short after all. We were able to talk all night. And as we became less afraid and more curious, we asked all the questions we wanted. And we found out lots of things.

We had guessed right. Iaia really was the farm owner's daughter. He was a guy named Sinho Peçanha, and Rosario had lived on the farm during the time of slavery. But she hadn't been a slave in a legal sense because she was born after the Free

Womb Law, the law that said slaves' children were born free.

But that law didn't really mean anything in the real world. Rosario's mother was a slave, and the farm owner said he wasn't going to support slaves' children for free. So when babies were born to his slaves, the master would threaten to leave them in the woods for the beasts to eat or drown them in the river. Then he wouldn't have to spend money supporting people he didn't own. The mothers would beg him to let their children stay at the farm with them, and he would agree in exchange for the child's future labor. So nothing changed for the slaves, except that on top of everything else, the little slave kids "owed one" to their master. And because they couldn't be sold to make a profit for their owner, they were treated even worse than the "real" slaves.

"They were no longer part of the estate's value," Leo explained, once he understood how the system worked.

"The same thing also happened to my grandmother, Galdina," said Rosario. "They passed a law against keeping old people as slaves. So when my grandmother turned sixty, Sinho Peçanha said that since she wasn't a slave anymore, he was no longer obliged by law to give her food and a place to live. So he threw her out. She hid in the woods and the next day came back and went with her daughter to talk to the mistress, the Sinha. The old woman cried and cried, my mother begged, and in the end the master agreed to let her go on living and eating there, but only as long as she kept on working."

"That's crazy! She sold her freedom for a dish of beans and rice," I said.

"Or did what she had to, to survive at any cost," said Leo.

"How horrible!" cried Tere in such a heartfelt way that I thought she would forget her fear of ghosts and hold Rosario's hand. But she didn't go that far.

"So this happened to all the slaves?" asked Leo.

"Here on this farm, to almost everybody. Every now and then some people, mainly men, decided to leave when they turned sixty to try to get a job in the city. But we never heard from them again and didn't know whether it had worked out or not. But most people stayed, begging, for God's sake, to remain a slave. Or they disappeared in the woods. Joana told us that on other farms, slaves were sometimes allowed to stay in a little house with a small piece of land, giving the master half of what they planted. But around here, Sinho Peçanha wouldn't let us."

"Who was Joana?" asked Elisa. "Was she the master's daughter?"

This time Rosario really smiled. A calm smile, as

though she was remembering something happy. You could see how beautiful she was when she didn't have that scared look. She had big, lively eyes (it's weird saying that about a dead girl, but it's true), and her smile made her look very interesting. Maybe she wasn't gorgeous, but she was beautiful. Especially when she was smiling with fond memories in her eyes.

I know it may be hard for you to imagine what she looked like. But believe me, it's even harder for me to describe her. Maybe this is one of the hardest things about being a writer, to have to use words as a camera to give a full portrait of someone.

I give up. I have to count on you to imagine a beautiful slave girl who lived in Brazil, back in the nineteenth century.

Anyway, Rosario went on explaining. "No, the master's daughter was named Iaia. Joana was my best friend. Such a wonderful friend! She was Ze Caboclo's daughter. He was a boatman who lived across the Rio Pardo river. When someone had to cross the river, they went to the dock, rang a bell, and he would come to pick them up in a little boat or canoe. That's why Ze Caboclo was so important to everybody. Only very rich and powerful people like Sinho Peçanha had their own boats and didn't need his services."

"What about the bridge?" asked Leo.

"What bridge?" said Rosario. "That little thing? You're mixing things up. That's on the Rio das Pedras, not on Rio Pardo."

That's how we found out that the old Rio Pardo bridge didn't exist back then. We thought it was so old that it had always been there.

But Rosario went on talking about her friend.

"Joana and her brother Bento were the only kids around who weren't either slaves or slave owners. They worked almost as hard as we did, helping with the chores at home. But they also had free time and could play. Once in a while they came to the *senzala* to talk. The master didn't like it. The overseer would yell at them and hit us. So sometimes we met them in the woods. Or at the edge of the river, where there is a big sapucaia tree hanging over a flat rock that has a sort of shelf at the back of it, like a bench. It was good for sitting on and hiding."

"I know where it is," said Leo.

"We like going there, too," said Elisa.

"That's where we went to meet when we could. Sometimes just Joana and me. Sometimes Amaro, my little brother, and Bento, her brother, came along as well. But after a while it became more and more difficult.

"Joana and Bento were doing something very

dangerous, and the two of us were helping them. We didn't want anyone to get suspicious. So it was especially important that the four of us not be seen together. At the very least it could lead to a really awful thrashing, the kind that almost tears your skin off. Or even worse it could endanger the thing we were doing."

We were curious. What dangerous thing? We asked a lot of questions. But Rosario began to act very strangely. On one hand, she didn't seem to want to talk, as if her mouth were locked. On the other hand, she went around and around, hinting at something, saying that she had to find a way to tell us. That this was something we needed to know, so that we could understand and help. Finally little by little, in answer to our questions, her secret came out.

I can imagine how difficult it was for her to explain all this to us. If I am having so much trouble telling you something that happened just a few months ago, how could a girl from another century and another world put all that she had gone through into words?

Rosario's story took place at the very end of the years of slavery. Because of the new laws, Sinho Peçanha, their master, couldn't buy any new slaves. Since trading in slaves had been forbidden, and the black market was being repressed, he was having trouble finding workers. This caused him financial problems, and he had to cut back on the number of guards who watched over the slaves. So every now and then a slave managed to escape. The best way to get away from the farm quickly was to go down to the edge of Rio das Pedras and then cross over and get away down the Rio Pardo. That's where Rosario's friends came in.

Ze Caboclo had made a new canoe and hardly ever used his old one anymore. It was kept ashore, hidden in the bushes at the edge of the river. So whenever an escape was about to take place, Rosario or Amaro found a way to let their friends know about it.

They had a complicated system. They draped a piece of cloth over a bush at the edge of the river, as if they had washed it and were putting it out to dry. It was risky, because usually people didn't go that far to do laundry, especially in the muddy waters of Rio Pardo when they had the crystal clear waters of Rio das Pedras nearby. But the boatman's children would see the sign and wait by that special rock beneath the sapucaia tree every afternoon between two and four, until Rosario or her brother managed to get away from work.

When they met up they would arrange where to leave the canoe hidden on this side of the river for the runaway to use, and where on the other bank the children could pick up the boat afterwards. They would also decide on the safest night for the escape.

This was their basic scheme. They had already helped with three escapes – one of them by an entire family. The master was getting more and more furious and violent. If he suspected the truth, he might have Rosario and Amaro killed.

"Killed?"

Tere could hardly believe it.

"Yes, killed. The master was very cruel. You have no idea how cruel," Rosario sighed. "I'm not sure I'll have the courage to tell you."

"He could do exactly what he liked, no matter how terrible. He had all the power and knew he wouldn't be punished by anyone," stated Leo. "And he probably could even use the argument that he had the law on his side."

We started to talk about the horrors of slavery. Rosario told us that she and her mother had been born in Brazil, on the farm.

But Grandma Galdina was still a child when she had been caught by an enemy tribe in Africa, tied up with ropes and taken to the shore, where she was sold to a dealer. She had told about the horrors of the sea journey in the hold of the ship, everybody crammed in, getting ill, barely able to move, lying in such filth with the horrible stench of vomit, piss, sweat, feces and infected wounds all mixed together. Fleas, cockroaches, lice, parasites of every kind and rats lived there, too. Because of these conditions, many of the prisoners died during the journey. Their bodies were thrown into the sea. Of course the survivors were whipped and treated horribly.

Grandma Galdina also told them that when they finally arrived in Brazil, they were taken to a market and "made beautiful" before being sold. That meant they were allowed to wash, comb their hair and remove the lice so that "the merchandise" could be sold for the highest price possible.

At the time of the auction they were offered for sale like animals. Often they were examined closely without any clothes on. The buyers tapped them to test their muscles, lifted their lips to examine their gums and teeth and tried to gauge their strength. Families were separated, sold off one by one to different owners, and often they never saw each other again.

I can't speak for my friends, but as I listened I felt so ashamed of being white and Brazilian. I had studied slavery in school, so what Rosario was saying wasn't exactly new. But it made me so mad, I couldn't even speak.

How can someone handle that, being so angry

about something and not being able to do anything? It was horrible to think about, impossible to imagine anything more terrible, unless you compared it to the stuff we saw in movies about what happened in the concentration camps during the Second World War. To think that human beings, people like us, could be so cruel. It was unbearable.

I think the four of us had similar feelings. Because suddenly Tere, who was crying, went and sat next to Rosario on the bed. She put her arms around her shoulders without saying a word. Our new friend hugged her back, and they cried together in each other's arms.

I immediately recognized the sound of sobbing and moaning that we had heard before, in the darkness. And I understood what it was about. It was sorrow, pain and suffering. The pain trapped inside the *senzala* walls sweated tears that ran through our souls.

I don't know how long we sat there. One by one we joined in the weeping, even Leo and I, I'm not at all embarrassed to say. It felt as though we were crying so that the memory of what happened would not be lost, so that nothing like that could ever happen again.

Suddenly we heard the rooster crow.

"The *carijó*!" Rosario said.

She started to become transparent, as if she were turning into steam. In a few seconds Tere was sitting there alone, in a very strange position, as if she were hugging the air. Rosario had disappeared.

I think that was the moment when I decided to tell more people about our meetings so that the memory of what Rosario had told us wouldn't disappear. And to try to do something to make sure that those things would never happen again.

But I didn't think it was going to be written down. Nor that Elisa would help me so much, revising the text, giving suggestions, using things she learned in her reading. That's why I'm able to do it now.

8

BLACK ON WHITE

WE GOT UP very late the next morning since we hadn't gone to bed until sunrise. And we were busy all day helping at the inn, because so many guests came that Saturday. Vera and my mom kept giving us chores.

At the end of the afternoon I was sitting on the porch tying a hook to a pole with a nylon string. I was making a fishing rod for one of the guests' little kids who wanted to go fishing the next day. Elisa came and sat next to me.

"Everyone is so busy, it looks like my grandmother won't be able to tell her story today," she said.

I looked at her, surprised. With all that was happening she wanted Granny to tell her bedtime stories?

"Iaia's story, the one she promised. Remember?" she explained.

"Of course." How could I have forgotten? Probably because I had a lot on my mind that day. I was thinking over all the things Rosario had told us.

But Elisa was right. It was impossible that day. Later when she looked for Dona Carlota to remind her of her promise, the old lady said, "Tomorrow, my darling, tomorrow. We can't today. Tomorrow is Sunday, most of the guests won't stay overnight. After supper, before you go to bed, we can sit on the porch and talk. Don't worry, I won't forget. I've been wanting to tell you this story. It's something you and Leo need to know."

We didn't mind. We had a lot to look forward to – a new meeting with Rosario. That is, if she came. But now we knew how to call her. Darkness, total silence in the house, Iaia's candlestick.

She came.

It was easier this time. Rosario wanted to join us so badly, she began to wander around when night fell. But she didn't need to cry or moan anymore, because now we knew the power of Iaia's candlestick, which Rosario herself had used so many times, so long ago, in that exact same place.

After everyone went to bed and the inn was completely silent, we had gathered in the Banana Leaf Saleswoman room, turned off the lights and lit the candle. We sat still, concentrating with all our strength, thinking hard about how we wanted

Rosario to appear. We'd admitted to each other that it wasn't just curiosity anymore. We were sympathetic. We wanted to help, though we didn't know how. But we were sure there must be a way, and we were going to find it. Rosario herself had suggested an answer when she said she had to tell us everything. But one key piece of the puzzle was still missing – the end of Rosario's story.

"What happened next is much worse than anything I've told you so far. It was truly like hell," she had announced the night before.

And when a ghost says something like that, you have to believe it. We found out that night. And it was impossible not to agree with Rosario's description. It was hell.

"What I'm going to tell you today is the story of the end," she said.

"The end of slavery?" asked Leo.

Rosario looked at all four of us before answering, a little like she had done the first night before she started talking. It was as if she were examining us, testing us to see if we were trustworthy. Or if we could handle the truth. Then she said, "The story of my end. Of how I died."

I never thought I would hear that verb used that way – in the first person in the past tense, without it being just a way of talking like, "I was so tired I almost died." In Rosario's mouth the word had real meaning, as it will one day for all of us, if we can do what she did – die, survive in some way, come back and then tell about it.

I don't know. I'm getting confused. But it's not easy, especially for someone who has never read or written much like me. I know that hearing her voice saying, "I died," just like that, so naturally, sent a chill up my spine. Maybe because I suddenly understood what a strong and weird experience we were having. We were talking to a dead person. Maybe because I felt that this was really, truly what life is all about. Death is just the other side of life. Everything that is alive has to die one day. But we don't like to think about death, to admit that it will come to us, too, and to all the people we love.

Anyway, I can't explain it, but what was happening stirred up all kinds of feelings, some of them not so pleasant. That's why I won't even try to use Rosario's exact words after this, though I've tried to up until now. But I don't know if I can do it anymore. I think not, so I'll just sum up what she told us. I'm leaving a lot of stuff for Elisa to help me with when she revises what I've written. This text that you are reading (I never know how many of you will read this) has already passed through her hands once. But I don't know if the two of us, even working together, will be able to tell the story exactly. I just know that Rosario went on something like this.

"We should have suspected. That day felt different right away, not because something had happened, but because of a tension in the air, a very strong..."

To hide my nervousness and weird feelings, I interrupted, "What do you mean?"

"Like the day of a storm before the wind begins and the rain falls. But without a storm. Do you see?"

We could see.

"Well, since early morning Amaro and I knew it would be a dangerous day, but that's not what I am talking about. It was dangerous because Doroteu, one of the slaves who picked the coffee, had been badly beaten. He couldn't take it anymore and decided to risk the worst. He decided to run away that very night, because there would be no moon. It was all settled.

"But the overseer must have suspected something. The day before we had seen him checking the riverbank very carefully, right by the place where Joana and Bento had agreed to bring the old canoe. So Amaro talked to Doroteu, and they decided that my brother would try to tell the boatman's children to leave the boat somewhere else. But we didn't know if Amaro would be able to reach them in time. So we were nervous enough because of this."

As she told the story Rosario seemed a bit scared and jumpy, especially when the wind made a noise outside. Even the exchange of looks between us seemed to frighten her. We had caught her mood and were getting very tense ourselves.

"Just after Amaro sneaked off and went inside the Free Wood, as he used to call the woods between the *senzala* and the river, Iaia came by. Usually when she wanted something she would send a message, and we would meet her near the main house. Not this day. She came in person. She appeared out of nowhere, skipping around and looking so pretty in her fine embroidered dress with an umbrella to protect her from the sun, almost as if she were a doll."

Rosario paused and looked over at us, but she didn't really seem to see us. She sighed. Maybe she wanted to remember better or was looking for the exact words to tell us what she remembered. Now that I'm trying to write, I know how hard this can be.

Later Leo said that Rosario's look made him feel that we were becoming transparent to her, that she seemed to look through us, at the wall. I don't know.

Elisa thinks she was just looking within, remembering, concentrating on something inside her.

Tere is sure she was looking at the Debret drawing behind us, as if she were searching for an umbrella to show us what fashion was like back then.

I don't know, as I have already said. All I know is that it was a strange pause, different from someone just taking a deep breath in the middle of a conversation.

Then she continued. "Everybody was working. The men were cleaning up the coffee trees, because the beans had been harvested and dried and were now ready to be roasted. The women had gone to the master's house or to the riverbank to do laundry or to feed the cattle. I should have been doing chores with them, but I pretended to have forgotten something and made up an excuse to stay near the *senzala* a little longer. I was worried about Amaro. Oh, my little brother, poor thing! He was only nine years old and was deep inside the Free Wood doing such a risky thing."

Maybe that was it. Perhaps Rosario's pause had been caused by sorrow and longing for her brother.

"What about Iaia?" asked Elisa very sweetly. I thought it was a way of distracting Rosario from the sad memories.

"Well, that was the amazing thing," she answered with a sigh. "Iaia had come over to talk to me, can you imagine? She was a nice girl. Sometimes she would play with me. She had given me a few things, and she almost always stood up for us when her father was angry. But she hardly ever came near the *senzala*.

"Well, on this day she came to tell me some news. Something incredible. We had heard rumors about it, but I never thought I'd be the first to find out that it was really true. The slaves who worked in the master's house and served the table had overheard bits of conversation when visitors came over. And they had told us at night in the *senzala* that everyone was talking a lot about abolition, the end of slavery. Maybe this time it might really come to pass.

"And indeed Iaia had come to tell me that the traveler, who had just spent the night at the house, told them that back in the capital city, almost two months before, a princess had signed a law. And that from that day on nobody was allowed to have slaves.

"Sinho Peçanha had argued with his guest saying that this didn't count because the emperor was the real ruler, and that no woman was going to make decisions about his estate and his goods, and other things like that. Iaia told me that the man just laughed and said that if her father didn't respect these orders and the law, he would be left with nothing. Because he didn't own slaves anymore – now everyone was free. And he could end up losing his lands, his coffee plantation, the houses and even risk going to jail if he didn't obey the law soon and release everybody – because the emperor had agreed with the princess and approved what she had done.

"Of course, Princess Isabel... the Gold Law," we

said, remembering what we had studied in history lessons at school. "That's it."

"But here, at the end of the world, we didn't know whether it was really true or not," continued Rosario. "So Sinho Peçanha ordered the overseer to saddle his horse that very evening and ride to the next village to find out exactly what had happened. When I heard what Iaia said, foolish me, I thought it was too good to be true. And then I thought, if the overseer was far away, Amaro was in less danger. My heart was beating so hard it seemed like it would jump out of my mouth. I was filled with the strongest feelings of fear and happiness I had ever felt in my life. Never to be a slave, ever again. Can you imagine?"

No matter how hard I try, I don't think I can really imagine exactly how she felt. I've always been free, so it's hard to know what it would be like to live as a slave. Slavery is such a terrible thing, it's beyond my imagination. To truly know how she felt, you would have to have been a slave, I think.

Rosario went on talking. "Iaia told me that the overseer had returned and confirmed the news the traveler had brought. He said that the people in the village had burst into laughter when they heard that Sinho Peçanha thought he still owned slaves.

The master's house was a mess. Iaia's father shouted, slammed doors, broke things, whipped the furniture, threatening this and that. Then he asked that all the slaves be gathered inside the *senzala* to listen to the news. When Iaia heard this she had snuck out and come running to tell me. No one had noticed her leave.

"By now it was obvious that the others were starting to hear the news, too. The slaves gathered from all around, dropping their tools, singing, laughing, dancing and clapping their hands. Women wiped their hands on their aprons. Men threw their hats in the air. Everybody was hugging. It was like a party!

Within minutes all the former slaves had gathered in the yard in front of the *senzala*. By the time the overseer arrived, only Amaro was missing. But the overseer didn't even notice. With all the confusion he couldn't do a head count.

"Then," Rosario continued, "he said that slavery was over and that Sinho Peçanha needed to talk to everybody and explain what it would be like from now on. He was going to tell them that he might even owe them money and surprising things like that. He wanted everyone to gather in the *senzala*, so that he wouldn't have to shout. Sinho Peçanha was worried that his words would be lost in the wind. Inside we would be able to hear what he had to say. So we went inside. Everyone was so happy.

"Once the last person was in, the overseer shut the door, locked it from the outside and put a huge log against it, blocking it shut. There was no way to get out. It was pitch dark inside, and we fell silent. It was eerie."

Now I'm coming to the hardest part of all to write, and I'll go quickly by the details, because I really can't handle this.

Rosario began with the silence in the dark and then said that they heard a voice. It was Sinho Peçanha's angry voice, shouting and cursing outside. He shouted that no one could do such a thing to him; that the government didn't have the right; that they couldn't put an end to his legacy just like that; that he had spent many years putting all this together, helping to produce the country's wealth; that he had paid a high price and wasn't going to lose it all without at least getting paid back.

I think that if it had happened these days, he would probably have brought up his "property rights," as we see in newspapers every time some group wants to maintain its privileges.

That's just my comment. I'm sorry, I shouldn't be giving opinions. It's just that I'm trying to put off telling what happened next. The things I don't want to tell, which I promised to tell, which can hardly be told.

The slaves, locked in the dark inside the *senzala*, heard the following order.

"Spread the oil!"

Then they could smell it. Soon after they felt the heat, saw light from a fire, heard the crackling of flames spreading quickly up onto the straw roof and then down into the room with them.

If he couldn't have slaves, Sinho Peçanha preferred to set them on fire. Burn everyone alive. So that at least freedom wouldn't be a party, and he wouldn't have to face the looks in the eyes of free black people.

But that's not how Rosario talked. She didn't say anything that sounded like a speech, a newspaper article or a history lesson. Staring almost blindly across the room, tears poured down her face as she sobbed and told us how it felt – the heat, the running, the screaming, the pain.

To tell you the truth, I don't really know what she actually said, or what I imagined. Most of all, I don't know what else there was that I couldn't even imagine, even with her telling us.

Let's just say the scene was like this: first the darkness with the smell of oil, very strong. Then almost at once, a really intense heat, and the sound of crackling as the fire spread over everything in its way.

But there are things I don't know, I don't remember or perhaps Rosario didn't even tell us. Honestly, I don't know if she actually talked about the flames – everything yellow, red and orange, growing every second, the fire licking everything in its way – or if

that's just stuff I've made up from seeing so many movies with fires in them.

One thing I'm sure of, Rosario talked about the smoke and how her eyes hurt, about the lack of air and about everybody screaming and coughing inside the *senzala*, running back and forth, some throwing themselves against the door. Some people fell and got trampled, but she stayed in a corner, hugging her mother. When I try to remember what she said, I'm not sure about the flames, but I'm sure about the smoke. Maybe she suffocated before she was burned and didn't feel the fire consume her flesh. But then again, maybe not. Maybe she did tell us, and I can't remember because I was too upset and shocked. Either way, it was hell.

"It seemed like it would never end. But then all of a sudden, it was over," she finished. "I died."

We were silent. Nobody could move or say anything, thinking of how the *senzala* must have looked then, full of smoke, piled with burnt bodies that no one could even identify.

Rosario herself was the first to speak.

"And I died thinking of Amaro, wishing I could warn him not to come back. If they did this to us, I imagined what they might do to my brother when they caught him — just a little boy helping a runaway slave. And all alone, with nobody to protect him or help him.

We were silent, unable to speak, as if there were a huge weight on us, or as if a part of each one of us had died there, too.

That's why it was a bit surprising to realize that as she finished her story, Rosario was actually asking for something.

"This is why I came. So that you can help me."

Elisa was the first one to pull herself together and answer, "Help? Of course! But how? What can we do?"

"Find out where Amaro is. And if he's alive, take care of him. Help him to get free."

The four of us looked at each other. Apparently Rosario didn't have any idea of the time that had passed and the impossible thing she was asking of us. The end of slavery had been in 1888. Even if her little brother had managed to escape and lived for many, many years, he would be dead by now. My God, what could we do? But we had to calm Rosario down, help her to live? Or die? Well, let's just say help her to be at peace. But we couldn't lie. What a situation!

The good thing is that in times like these Tere lets her heart speak. This was how she showed how much she cared, while the rest of us were desperately thinking about what we should do.

Tere went over to Rosario and put her arms around her. "Calm down, sweetheart, calm down. Nothing bad can happen anymore."

"But it's not just me. It's everybody."

"Leave it to us. We'll find a way. There, there, calm down. Nothing more can harm you now."

That was obvious. But what could we do to help?

"That's right," said Elisa. "We will find out what happened to your brother. But I'm sure nothing happened. Otherwise you would know, don't you think?"

She had a point. Rosario seemed calmer.

"And as soon as we know something, we'll tell you."

"No," Rosario said firmly. "That won't be possible. I'm not coming back. I have told you everything. Now it's up to you."

She got up and started walking around the room, her feet sliding as if they weren't really touching the floor. At first she moved slowly. Then she started to go faster. Faster and faster. Then she was spinning around and around. Just looking at her made us feel dizzy. Rosario was spinning and spinning, like a top – faster, faster, faster.

Trying to interrupt, Elisa called, "Rosario!" And then, "How can we help?"

Rosario suddenly stopped, pointed at me and said, "Mariano, promise you will help me? Do you swear?"

Her finger was pointing at me. I had no choice but to swear. "I promise."

I think Leo was jealous because he complained, "Why don't you pick me?"

"You already carry an obligation," she said.

Then she explained what she wanted. When she was finished she said to me, "Don't forget. Now you're a slave to your promise. It's a serious oath. Black ink on white paper."

How could I ever forget?

9

ALL RIGHT, I'LL WRITE

AFTER SHE had told her story, chosen me by her crazy spinning and forced me to promise to do what she wanted, Rosario became calm. She was quiet for a while, and so were we as we thought about what we had heard.

An owl hooted outside. Or a *bacurau*, I'm not sure. But it was a night bird. It was as if it were trying to remind us that the night went on, that life went on.

"I think today I will be able to leave before the *carijó* sings," she said. "I need to rest."

We understood. She did, and so did we.

"You're really not coming back?"

"Not this way. I mean, I don't need to anymore. I've passed everything on to you. And you will find out where my brother is. Take some flowers to his grave, pray for him. But you are right. He must not have had a violent death. His soul isn't wandering around. And I also don't need to worry about the rest, either. I'm sure you'll find a way to bring some kind of justice. You will tell everyone what Sinho Peçanha did and help to make sure that this doesn't happen ever again. That's why I can go and rest. And you won't see me. But I'll be around, taking care, watching over you."

"Like a guardian angel?" asked Elisa.

"Sort of," she smiled. "Me and the others, too. Many little angels all around, like the ones in the clouds at the feet of the Virgin of the Immaculate Conception, in the painting in the master's house."

I started to imagine a bunch of little black angels. Why not? Why do we always have to picture blond angels just because some painters in Europe so many centuries ago had imagined it that way? In Brazil we are all so mixed. And people who aren't born with dark skin soon become at least a bit dark from the sun. Even angels would. And of course little black and tan angels would know and understand us much better.

Rosario was saying goodbye. She was starting to get lighter, more transparent, turning into smoke. We already knew what this meant. And this time, she didn't even wait for the *carijó*'s call.

"God bless you," we heard as she vanished.

"God bless you, too!" answered Tere. "Have a good trip!"

Honestly, for someone who was always so afraid of ghosts, Tere was being very forward. Almost too forward, I thought. As if she were showing off or jealous that I was the chosen one, in charge of such an important mission.

But none of us said another word. Only good night. We were all exhausted and couldn't wait to get to sleep.

I can't speak for the others, but I had a strange dream that I can't remember properly. It started with fire and slaughter, prisoners escaping, ghosts dragging chains, fire and shadow, umbrellas made of white lace and angels with tanned skin, a dream full of stuff. But then there was a kind of emptiness with just a few things that stuck out. Smoke coming from coal burning on the ground, white smoke rising up toward the clouds in the sky; a dark wood table, partly covered by a white embroidered napkin, and on it a plate of food – black beans and rice; a teacup and two bowls – coffee and cream; dominoes, black with white spots; a *carijó* with speckled white and black feathers; an open book, black ink on white paper.

I woke up feeling very troubled and confused. I was thinking about all that had happened. About everything we had heard since Rosario appeared for the first time. About the story she had told. About my oath, a commitment to another world. About the dream and the promise.

It took me a while to get up, but I didn't worry too much because I saw that Leo was still sound asleep on the bed next to mine. I thought the girls would have been up long before and would be talking on the porch or down by the river. But when we finally came out of our room around lunchtime, they still hadn't left theirs.

"You almost missed lunch," said my mother. "I bet you were up to something until late last night."

I grinned, while Vera said, "I'll go wake up Elisa. This is a bit too much."

We were all very tired. We had slept so little the past few nights. Not to mention trying to sort out our thoughts. There was too much going on in our minds.

We only had a chance to talk much later. After a heavy lunch (Sunday was *feijoada* day), the four of us were still quite lazy. We didn't even leave the house. We lay around on the porch, the girls in a hammock and us on the floor. Leo asked the question I had been asking myself all along.

"Do you think you'll be able to keep your promise, Mariano?"

"I don't know, but I have to try."

"I'm glad she didn't choose me. I wouldn't be able to do it."

"Well, I think you should have been the chosen one," said Tere. "In fact, I don't understand why it was Mariano."

"What? Don't you think I can do it?" I asked, a bit offended.

"No, of course I do," she explained hesitating. "But it's just that Leo is a bit darker. Especially when we see Dona Carlota's skin color. He seems more likely to be descended from slaves. So he's the one who should have had the mission to speak for his ancestors."

"Maybe that's exactly why Rosario said he already carries that obligation," I reminded her.

"Yeah. She did say that. But she picked you. That's what I can't understand."

I didn't completely understand it, either. Fortunately Elisa came up with an explanation and a pretty logical one, too.

"Tere, for a black person or a mulatto – someone from mixed blood like Leo and I – being against slavery is the most natural thing in the world. Our ancestors were the ones who were slaves. We can never forget it. But you were the ones who enslaved us, and your job is to remember that all the time."

"Also when a black person talks about slavery, people don't pay much attention," said Leo. "Everyone sort of expects us to go on about it. But if the person who fights for this issue has fairer skin, maybe people will listen more. They might be more effective or at least get more attention. Don't you agree, Mariano?"

"Yeah. It could be. I never thought about it much. I just know it's going to be really hard. I don't actually like reading, I'm not used to writing, and I never stopped to think about these things. What I really like is to play computer games, play soccer and go fishing. That's why I think Rosario made the wrong choice. I'm not the right person for it."

"What about me?" asked Leo. "Don't I like the same things? And listening to music and riding my bike. Why should we, whose race has already suffered so much in this country, still have to do all the fighting? We should be allowed to take a break. It's break time, my brother. Go write your book while I go fishing. Look, I think Rosario knew very well what she was doing when she let me off the hook. I think this oath of yours is a punishment. We've already been punished enough. It's your turn, pale face."

Everyone laughed, but we knew it wasn't just a joke. There was some truth in what Leo was saying.

Then Elisa spoke up. "Actually, Mariano, you're not all alone in this. Leo and I also have a lot of "pale face" in us. Because if Grandma Carlota is really brown, our grandpa wasn't. And as for our grandparents on our dad's side! Remember, Leo? They were so white, if they went out in the sun without a hat they ended up looking like two red peppers. Poor things, they had such delicate, fair skin."

"It wasn't their fault, Elisa. They came directly from Italy to pick coffee beneath this hot, hot sun."

"I know. They were as white as paper. So based on your theory, we have to take on half the punishment, too. We'll help you, Mariano."

"Okay, I was joking. I'll help," agreed Leo. "I actually want to help. My white part is sympathetic and wants to show my solidarity. But my black part wants to have a choice, the freedom to go and have fun while Mariano works. It's not just being selfish. It's wanting the right to feel free. I'll help, but I don't want all the responsibility or to feel that it's an obligation. And I'm still glad that Rosario didn't choose me. I wouldn't be able to do it. Writing is too hard."

"Don't be silly, Leo," Elisa said. "Anyone can do it. You just have to sit down and start. Every day you write a little bit. Slowly but steadily – no rushing – and then one day it's ready."

"How do you know?"

"Well, I don't really know. But I think it must be that way."

Leo couldn't resist a tease. "Your problem is you think too much."

"You two aren't going to start now, are you?" interrupted Tere.

I was glad she had. Because I wanted to talk

about my promise to Rosario, and they were changing the subject.

I said, "But I can't do this without help from all of you. I don't even know if I paid enough attention. What if I mix things up or get confused or leave out something important?"

"Don't worry, we'll help you. I'll correct your words, give you ideas, do whatever I can. But you're the one who has to write it, because that's what you promised. You'll be doing it for all of us."

"Especially for Rosario, Amaro and the others," reminded Tere, "just like she asked. Even for the slaves we don't know anything about, so that there will never be slavery again."

"But it's not like there are any slaves today. Slavery was abolished."

"I don't know, Leo. Was it, really? I mean, everywhere? Forever?" I asked. "We studied abolition in history class, but every now and then on TV there's news about some guys who are working somewhere without getting paid. Or who can't leave because they owe the boss's store more than they receive in salary. I was thinking about that when I woke up this morning."

"Don't you remember? Just the other day there was something about a ship full of children sold to work on cocoa plantations that sailed near the coast of Benin," said Tere. "And on the Internet there's stuff about movements against slave work in some country or other all the time."

"What about the people who work around here in such poor conditions that it's not that different from the time of slavery?" added Elisa.

Leo agreed. "Yeah, you guys are right. I hadn't stopped to think about it. But now I understand that when Rosario asked us to tell her story, she wanted everyone to know so that it would never happen again. But Mariano's the one who's a slave to his promise."

We all laughed. I knew he was kidding and that the three of them would help me.

"All right, I'll write it," I said.

"But Mariano's commitment is only half of what she wanted," remembered Elisa. "The other half is a job for all of us. And that's much harder. How are we going to find out what happened to Amaro? And take flowers to his grave?"

That silenced us. Frankly, I had forgotten all about it. I had enough to worry about with the weight of my promise to write a book – to remember Rosario's whole story and put it on paper, black on white, as she requested.

My God, there was so much black and white. In my dream and in the story. Maybe one of the hardest things about this was that it wasn't just about slavery – an economic thing, an inhuman and immoral way to treat people and get free labor. The slaves weren't white. And the owners weren't black. So it was about skin color and race, too. It was really complicated. It was about an injustice so great that you couldn't get rid of it by just passing a law.

"Let's go around asking. Perhaps somebody's heard about this Ze Caboclo or his children," said Leo.

At first I didn't even know what he was talking about because I was so caught up in my own thoughts.

"Or we could try and find out his last name and look for information in some government bureau in Cachoeirinha," suggested Tere.

"How?"

"Some news about deaths in a newspaper from back then, for example. Or a grave in the cemetery with his name. Or some document at a notary's office. It might be hard work, but that's how it's done," said Elisa, who was always reading detective stories and had some idea about how to start.

"Yeah," I agreed, already feeling a bit depressed about all the work that was facing us.

Elisa noticed and let me off the hook.

"No. You're out of this. Since you have to write, leave the research to us. Your job is based so much on your memory, you can't run the risk of forgetting. Actually, it would be good if you got going right away while it's all fresh in your mind. The best thing would be to start today."

"Today?" I repeated, hardly believing she could be serious.

"Or tomorrow. And Leo and I will go to a notary's office to try to get some information."

All that effort to look for a needle in a haystack was freaking me out. I think Leo had a similar reaction, because he tried to gain some time.

"But we don't even know his last name yet. How will we be able to look?"

"There are some threads we can follow. Amaro isn't such a common name. And I've heard that often slaves were registered under their master's last names, so we could start checking whether there was someone named Amaro Peçanha."

"Or use my last name," said Tere.

"Yours?" we asked, surprised.

"Yes. My last name is Silva. Once I mentioned to my father that it was such a common name. He said that in the olden days, when they didn't know someone's family name, they often registered the child as "da Silva," which means "from the jungle" or "from the woods." Or they used "Santos," which means saints, or "Nascimento," which means birth. It was a way of saying that there was no family before, it started with this birth, or that it was up to the saints."

"Wow, that's interesting!" said Elisa. "I never heard that before. What I know is that when the Jews were persecuted in Portugal and had to convert so that they wouldn't be arrested, they changed their names to sound Christian. They adopted last names from trees they had in their backyards or from animals they liked or admired."

"So you think we should look up all the names of trees and animals in the notary's office?" asked Leo.

"What's the matter with you? Were you asleep? Amaro wasn't Jewish. I was just making conversation. But I do think we can try and find information about Amaro Peçanha, Amaro Nascimento, Amaro Santos and Amaro da Silva – someone who was born around 1879, because he was a nine-year-old boy at the time of abolition in 1888."

"And maybe he died that very year when captivity ended," I said.

"But then it's almost hopeless," said Leo. "A little black boy dying at a time like that. He would just disappear. There would be nothing about him in a newspaper. In fact, there probably weren't any newspapers in Cachoeirinha back then. Anyway, it will be really hard. A kid dying in the middle of all that confusion? They would bury him without even a gravestone."

"But there might have been some kind of record of a burial. The cemetery might be a good place to start."

"And what kind of mischief are you children up to now? Are you planning to make trouble in the cemetery?"

We didn't even have to turn around to know that this interruption came from Dona Carlota, who had crept up silently behind us. She was the only person we knew who would still use the word "mischief."

Leo quickly got up and brought over a chair for his grandmother to sit on. Often after the last guest had left on Sunday afternoons, she would come and talk to us until dinnertime. Dinner usually included Tere's grandparents, too, when they came by to pick her up. Sometimes I couldn't stay because my dad liked to go back to Cachoeirinha early, especially when there was a soccer match on TV. He liked to watch the game at home. But this Sunday we had all stayed.

After Dona Carlota was comfortably seated, leaning against a cushion Elisa had brought with her legs stretched out on a little stool, I thought she would ask again about the cemetery. But I was wrong.

"I owe you something, and I have come to pay my debt," she announced.

"Iaia's story!" Elisa remembered.

I confess I had forgotten about it myself.

"That's right."

But before she could even begin, Elisa impatiently launched into her research. "I'm sorry, Grandma,

but have you ever heard about a guy named Ze Caboclo who used to live around here? Or one of his children or grandchildren?"

Dona Carlota thought for a while, but the name meant nothing to her.

"What about Amaro Peçanha? Or Amaro da Silva? Or do Nascimento or dos Santos?"

"No, I never heard of anyone called those names, either." She paused and then added, "But would

Amaro de Andrade do any good? He was my grand-father."

We all broke out with questions at the same time. Even we couldn't hear what we were saying. Was it just a coincidence? Was it the same Amaro we were searching for? But how? Dona Carlota's grand-father?

"If you'll all be quiet and let me speak, I will tell you his story."

"His story or Iaia's story?"

"It's the same, Elisa, the same story. And it's also our story, the story of our family, of this place and this inn."

There! One more thing I'll have to write about for you. That was my first reaction. This is never-ending work. Writers have no rest. I had no choice. I had to pay attention.

"Many, many years ago, back when we still had an emperor, this place was part of a huge farm, much bigger than this ranch. There was a lot of land. Land that stretched out on all sides, so far that a man on a horse couldn't cross it all in one day. Really enor-mous. A prosperous and powerful farm with a large house full of stylish furniture, an imported piano, French china, English silverware, Belgian embroi-dered towels and linen, and much more. The source of all this wealth was the huge coffee plantation that spread out as far as the eye could see."

"And the slave labor that the eye couldn't see," I said interrupting. I don't even know why I had, but I think I was already starting to put my ideas into place for when the time came for me to write.

"Exactly!" confirmed Dona Carlota, giving me a long look as if she were really seeing me for the first time. "The owner of this farm was a very cruel man who thought he was above the law. He owed no account of his actions to anyone. He did whatever he wanted, certain that he was so powerful and lived so far from the capital city that he would never be punished. It was as if in this place, so far from everything, he was the law, the jury and the executioner. He was cruel to the slaves and oppressive to the women at home. Several thugs worked for him. If he wanted, he could have his enemies killed during the night. Some people called him Peçonha, which means poison – that's how bad he was."

"But his real name was slightly different. It was Peçanha, wasn't it?" asked Tere.

"I don't know. All I know is what my father told me, which I am now telling you. But if you children want him to have a name, we can call him Coronel Peçanha."

"Can we call him Sinho Peçanha?"

"Yes, son, yes. Anyway, let me tell you the story. This farmer thought there was no limit to his power, no limit at all. But one day he heard news that slavery had ended in Brazil and that he couldn't own people anymore. And since he had boasted about his evil deeds, a traveler who had spent the night at the farm made a veiled threat to denounce him to the authorities.

"Finally powerful Coronel Peçanha was afraid, perhaps for the first time in his life. Perhaps it was this combination of fear of punishment and the rage he felt at losing his power that upset him so much. But he completely lost his mind. And then this Sinho Peçanha, as you want me to call him, committed an act of sheer madness, one that made all his previous acts of cruelty seem like nothing. When he heard he could not have slaves anymore, he gathered all the former captives in the *senzala* using some excuse."

"He said he would explain what their freedom meant. And he even implied that he owed them some money," said Elisa.

"That could be. I don't know. But we can imagine that was how it went," agreed Dona Carlota. "Anyway, what I do know is that he locked all his former slaves inside the *senzala*. And then he ordered his thugs to set the building on fire and burn everyone inside — men and women, old people and children. They all died."

"Nobody escaped?"

"How could they escape? The place had no windows, the roof was made of straw and soon caught fire, and the only door was barred. It was a massacre. His wife and daughter watched the whole thing in horror. The overseer went mad. He couldn't bear it and ran into the woods screaming, never to be seen again. He must have been crazy already, because no decent human being could do such a thing."

Dona Carlota paused, looked around and went on.

"But they did not know that one of the children from the farm had managed to escape. He had been on the bank of Rio Pardo talking to some friends – a boatman's children. They saw the smoke from afar and came running. Hiding in the woods, they saw

the whole thing. The boy wanted to scream and run to his family – his mother, his sister and his grandmother were being burnt alive in that hell. But his friends grabbed him and wouldn't let him go.

"In the end they took him back to their house on the other side of the river. They helped him get away so that the farmer wouldn't find him. Their father went to the nearest village and talked to the teacher at the local school, who was moving to a distant town. He was a good man. When the teacher heard the boy's story, he felt such pity that he decided to take care of the boy himself. He registered the child under his own name, as if he were his own son, and took him to the new town where he was going to live. That's how my grandfather got an education. But the teacher helped him even more than that."

"What did he do? You mean that before they left he went by the farm and kicked Sinho Peçanha's butt?" said Leo.

"No. Before leaving, he reported the case to the court. He did not reveal the boy's identity, but he brought a charge against Sinho Peçanha. And later when the teacher was settled in the other town, he wrote giving his address and said that he would like to follow the trial from afar.

"Because of his charge, the authorities decided to follow up. They went to the farm and saw the ruins of the burnt-down *senzala*. Sinho Peçanha denied the charges and said the fire had been an accident. He pretended that the *senzala* had been empty at the time of the fire, saying that the former slaves had left the farm long before. He also invented many other stories. But his power had weakened. The overseer was missing. Many of his thugs had decided it was better to disappear as well. Finally there was evidence, and there were witnesses – the boatman's children and even Sinho Peçanha's daughter testified against him."

"Iaia?"

"Exactly. That was Iaia, how did you guess? She was very brave, and her testimony was decisive. The police took the farmer to jail that very day. They talked about sending him to be judged at the capital city's court or something like that. But he never came to trial. He died that very night. It was certainly not from remorse, but maybe because of anger or despair at being powerless for the first time. Who knows? The humiliation of prison was too much for someone like him. He had a stroke in prison, and nobody came to help."

"Serves him right!"

"Good. Because if he had escaped, poor Iaia would have had to pay," said Elisa.

"But in a way, Iaia did pay," said Dona Carlota.

"How could she pay? How could a dead man punish or beat up his daughter?"

"Iaia didn't get punished for helping to put him in jail. I'm talking about a different kind of payment, many years later. And if you stop interrupting so much, perhaps I can finish the story."

"Tell us, tell us!" we asked.

Leo's grandmother continued. "That huge farm was left to Iaia and her mother. There were no more slaves to plant and harvest the coffee, to roast the beans or grind them. Nor to milk the cows, feed the chickens, do the laundry, cook the meals, clean the house, fix the fences or do all the other hard work a place like that requires.

"Inside the house they could still get along, because even rich women have always worked a lot. And so they cooked food, sewed clothes, prepared sausages, took care of the animals in the yard, and so on.

"But it was impossible for them to take care of the farm. In the beginning they tried hiring employees, but they didn't know how to manage them. And the money started to run low. Soon they had to abandon the coffee plantation.

"Everything was in decline. They started selling off what they had in order to survive. Little by little they divided the farm and sold the land, until all that was left was just this part around the house, which is now our ranch.

"After a few years Iaia's mother died, and Iaia was

left alone and sad. They say that she didn't want to go out and locked herself inside the house. She never married, but not due to a lack of candidates. She was beautiful and had some money. But people said she was disturbed forever by the fire in the *senzala*. We can't be sure. What we do know is that she lived locked in the master's house with few employees, selling the precious objects from the house little by little — the carpets, the jewelry, the most valuable furniture, the silverware, the dishes that weren't yet broken. She died young after months of being terribly sick. She was not much older than twenty."

Dona Carlota sat quietly, looking at the sky, which was slowly becoming darker. Only one star shone brightly. We understood what she meant when she said that Iaia had paid. It was as if the poor girl had paid with her life for her father's evil deeds. It was a sad story with a sad ending. I don't like stories like that.

"Is that all?" asked Elisa. She, too, was disappointed with the story that we had been promised and that we had waited for, for so long. "What about your grandfather, Amaro?"

"Wait, I haven't come to that part yet," said Dona Carlota.

I was glad that there was still more to come.

She went on. "After Iaia died, they found out she had left a will. It was a surprise. Next to it there was a letter in which she said that the boatman's children had told her that a little boy had escaped on that terrible day. He was the brother of a slave girl whom she liked very much. Iaia only knew that his name was Amaro. But she made him her only heir and requested that all efforts be made to track him down.

"It was not easy. The only ones who knew Amaro were the boatman's family, and they no longer lived there. But the terrible story of the fire had shocked many people in the region. Everyone felt they had to help somehow. And it was a good thing they did, because I don't believe the authorities would have made much effort to find a little black boy to make him an heir. But someone ended up finding one of the boatman's children, who revealed the secret of the escape and told them the boy had been adopted by the old school teacher. Then the search for the teacher began. He had left the other town, retired and gone to live in the capital city. Nobody knew where. But in the capital there were newspapers where they put an advertisement requesting that Amaro de Andrade present himself to the authorities of Cachoeirinha to deal with a matter in his own interest."

"And so he came running home?"

"Not really, no. He saw the ad because he could read, but he was very suspicious. At first he thought of running away. But he talked to one of his foster brothers, a lawyer who offered to go with him, arguing that it could be to testify about Sinho Peçanha. They did not know that he had died. So they came. And to Amaro's total surprise, what awaited him was the ownership of the old farm – or at least the house, the yard and a small piece of land around it, because there was not much left beyond that."

Okay, now the story ended!

"And that's how this ranch ended up in my family's hands, inherited from Iaia by my grandpa, Amaro."

"My great-grandfather?" asked Leo.

"No, your great-great-grandfather."

"Does that mean that Rosario is my great-great aunt?"

Dona Carlota answered with another question.

"Who is Rosario?"

The four of us looked at each other, not knowing how to answer. Finally Elisa said, "Amaro's sister."

"And how did you find out about her?"

Nobody dared answer. How could we ever explain the whole thing?

"You children are acting very mysterious. You've been up to something. Come on, tell me," she insisted.

Luckily, at that exact moment, Tere saw her grandparents' car arrive, and the conversation was interrupted by dinner. But before we all went running out into the garden, Dona Carlota said, "Today you have escaped. But you do owe me Rosario's story. I told you Iaia's."

"Okay, Grandma," Elisa promised. "We'll tell you. But it will take a while, and it's going to be written down."

There, you see? It was up to me again. Not only did I have to write because I was a slave to a promise made to a ghost (as I never properly explained, but I'm sure you understand by now), but I also had to show what I wrote to someone else's grandmother. Oh, my God! Why did these things keep happening to me?

That's why I spent months sitting in front of a computer, trying to remember all this and figuring out how best to tell it. Every day I wrote a little. First it came out as one big chunk of information, like a very long assignment at school. When I showed it to my friends they thought it should be more like a book, with chapters and titles and stuff like that. And even illustrations, which Leo was left in charge of making. And Elisa wrote almost the whole thing all over again with her many suggestions. To make it more interesting, she said. I don't know. I'm not very good at doing this. The others were the ones who ended up making suggestions and choosing everything. They even tried to pick the book's title. But I chose another name and a very important one.

A few weeks ago I had finally given the book to

Dona Carlota and our parents to read. Without this part at the very end, which I'm writing now, of course.

Last night when we gathered on the porch before Sunday dinner, my parents and Vera were there, too. They praised me for what I had written, but we could tell that they didn't really believe what they had read – except for Dona Carlota. They thought that we showed a lot of imagination and said some nice things about my way of writing. They were especially curious about where I had gotten all these ideas. And they laughed when I said it was from memory. But not Dona Carlota.

In the end she said, "Well, now we need to choose

a name for the inn, and I think we can find it in this story. What do you suggest? What about Grandpa Amaro's Ranch?"

That wasn't a name for an inn. We weren't too excited.

"Maybe Saint Amaro Inn," said Vera.

"Or Iaia's Inn," said my mother.

"Yes," my father agreed. "That has good commercial appeal. It suggests a trip to the past, a traditional weekend. It's probably a good way to attract guests."

"No, this has to be a homage to the slaves, not the masters!" said Leo decisively, and everyone saw that he was right.

"Rosario's Inn," was Elisa's suggestion.

"No, that sounds weird. What about The Senzala Inn?"

"That's kind of depressing," said Leo. "What about you, Mariano? Don't you have any ideas?"

"Free Wood Inn," I said, shyly.

"Hey, that's a good idea. It's the brand on my candlestick, which belonged to Rosario and Iaia," said Elisa.

"I wasn't even thinking of that," I explained. "I was thinking about the name Amaro gave to the woods. And it goes well with this place, because we still have a small wood that we want to preserve."

"And a lot of freedom that we also want to preserve," completed Leo.

"And I swore that by writing about what happened, I would help to remember it forever, so that nobody forgets," I said.

And so it was. And if you're ever traveling around here and pass by Cachoeirinha, come and visit us. Free Wood Inn. It's small, but lovely. Now guaranteed to be ghost-free. I am sure you'll like it.

HISTORY

THE STORY in this book takes place in Brazil, a country that constitutes nearly half of Latin America and is the only Portuguese-speaking country in the Americas. Part of what is told here happened in the nineteenth century, and it may be useful to know more of the history of that time.

In 1808 Napoleon Bonaparte, the French emperor, conquered many countries in Europe and invaded Portugal. His armies were very powerful, and he had defeated all his enemies up to then. In order to escape him and avoid having to surrender, the Portuguese king decided to move his whole court to one of his colonies, Brazil. So a huge fleet was prepared in a hurry, and the entire government moved from Lisbon to a new capital city, Rio de Janeiro – not only the king and the aristocracy, but also bankers, businessmen and artists. They took works of art and the wonderful collection from the royal library with them.

Some years later when the danger of Napoleon had receded, the king returned to Portugal, leaving his son Pedro as his representative in Brazil. The colony became independent in 1822 but remained under the rule of that same prince, who was acclaimed Emperor Pedro I.

From colonial times the country's economy had been based on the work of slaves. All the wealth that came from gold and diamond mines or sugar cane plantations was produced by African slaves. But in Brazilian society there was at the same time a good deal of racial blending. The Portuguese mixed with the Africans and the native Americans. Very soon most people were of mixed race. The anti-slavery movements became stronger and stronger. Increasingly there were rebellions, and runaway slaves sometimes established their own free territories. But the slave owners were also very powerful and influential in the parliament. So instead of putting an end to slavery once and for all, the senators and representatives passed a series of laws gradually restricting it.

The whole process was painfully slow and drawn-out. In 1850 it was forbidden to bring new slaves from Africa. The ships that brought them were chased by the navy, but it was a very long coast and there were always a lot of smugglers. In 1864 Emperor Pedro II set free all the slaves that worked for the government. In 1871 the so-called Free Womb Law declared that all slaves' children born from that date on were free. In 1885 another law gave freedom to those who were over sixty-five. Finally in 1888, while the emperor was away, his daughter, Princess Isabel, signed a document called the Gold Law, and slavery in Brazil came to an end. The slave owners were so angry and caused so much political turmoil that in the following year, 1889, the emperor was ousted. The country officially became a republic, ruled by a president, as it is today. But from then on slavery was illegal in Brazil.

GLOSSARY

Bacurau – A Brazilian nighthawk.

Baiana – A slave born in the province of Bahia whose traditional white dress included a lacy or embroidered blouse, a shawl, a turban and lots of colorful necklaces, bracelets and gold pendants.

Carijó – A breed of hen with black and white speckled feathers.

Feijoada – A popular Brazilian dish made of black beans boiled with pork, served with rice and manioc meal, which comes from the tropical cassava plant.

Mucama – A slave who worked in the master's house and typically wore a long cotton skirt and a full, short-sleeved blouse.

Mulatto – A person from mixed black and white descent.

Senzala – The slave quarters on a plantation.